a Shot WITH you

A BOURBON BROTHERS
ROMANTIC COMEDY

A BOURBON BROTHERS
ROMANTIC COMEDY

TERI ANNE STANLEY

Entangled Publishing, LLC
2614 South Timberline Road
Suite 109
Fort Collins, CO 80525
Visit our website at www.entangledpublishing.com.

Lovestruck is an imprint of Entangled Publishing, LLC.

Edited by Robin Haseltine
Cover design by Bree Archer
Cover art from iStock

Manufactured in the United States of America

First Edition January 2017

For Tom, thanks for thinking to marry me twenty-five years ago so we could do research on our anniversary trip!

Chapter One

Brandon Morgan stood in front of the Travel Adventures office in Puerto Vallarta and stared down at Mexico's youngest extreme watersports guide.

Nope.

Call him Mr. Excitement with as much sarcasm as you like, but he was on vacation, and he'd choose the fun. The "high adventure" he'd signed up for was as appealing as a trip to the dentist. For fillings. Without anesthetic. And it was *his* vacation, damn it. If he had to leave his cozy, air-conditioned stateroom and its wifi connection, he was going to live it up in a way that made *him* happy.

By working.

He looked at the kid and said, "Sorry, bud. I think I'm gonna contribute to my life insurance for a few more years. I'll pass on ski-surfing today."

"But *senõr*, you've already paid for the trip. If you join the tequila tour, you'll have to pay again." *And I'll lose the generous tip you'd give me for bringing you back alive. If I bring you back alive.*

At least that's what Brandon figured he meant, so he gave the kid a few bucks and escaped into the liquor store that had a sign reading, "TEQUILA TOUR! CRUISE GUESTS WELCOME!"

Before he reached the smiling attendant behind the counter, a familiar label caught his eye: BLUE MOUNTAIN BOURBON, DANGEROUS DAVE'S EIGHT BALL. *Sweet.* His distribution team had managed to get it out, right on time. It wasn't available on the ship, so he snatched a bottle from the shelf and carried it back to the cashier.

"This bottle, and one ticket for the tequila tour." He could skip the tequila tasting—yech—and have bourbon. No cactus water for him.

"You'd better hurry, *amigo*," the attendant told him. "The bus is leaving."

Brandon threw a handful of bills at the guy and sprinted from the shop, across the crumbling roadway, and leaped onto the bus filled with grinning, sunburned tourists.

As the doors shut behind him, he fell into an empty seat next to an elderly woman with purple hair. She didn't glance away from the iPad she held to the window, videoing the scenery, which in this case, consisted of a broken-down truck in front of a store claiming to have "Authentic Aztec silver jewelry at rock bottom closeout prices." Brandon would have to remember to stop by there to pick up something for his mom's birthday. Mom would appreciate authentic rock-bottom-discounted jewelry. After all, she'd loved—and still occasionally wore—the vending machine plastic gemstone ring he'd given her when he was eight.

The bus jerked with a hiss of air brakes and jolted forward.

"Welcome to the Pequeño Zarigüeya tour! Sit back and enjoy the ride as you enjoy these hits of Mexican radio." The music that fuzzed through ancient speakers was nothing that had been produced before his parents were in diapers, but then, he wasn't a big connoisseur of south-of-the-border pop.

Maybe they *did* play a lot of Herb Alpert and the Tijuana Brass here these days.

He'd made the right choice to bail on the extreme sports and could instead fantasize about mergers and acquisitions to his heart's content. He slid the bottle of bourbon into his drawstring backpack and tucked it between his knees, grateful to have escaped another freaking *adventure*.

Gramps had challenged Brandon to "get the hell off the cruise ship and do something interesting. Meet some women instead of hiding in your cabin to work, for Chrissakes," so for the last few stops he'd done things that his family and friends deemed exciting. He'd gone on a zip line tour of the rain forest in Costa Feo. And spent the next day swallowing Advil. He'd gone kayaking down the Rio Tehuantepec and wound up with mosquito bites the size of dinner plates. At least he was pretty sure he didn't have Zika virus, always a bonus. Plus, he could check "Stretch outside of comfort zone" off of his corporate leadership self-improvement list. But he'd had enough.

This distillery tour—this was what interested him. He wouldn't pretend that he was going to drink instead of work—as one of the sons of a prize-winning bourbon distilling family, sniffing samples of tequila and touring a distillery *was* work. It was market research and checking out the competition, and he loved it.

"Hey! You. Mr. Cutie Drawers!"

Brandon grunted when a sharp elbow dug into his ribs.

He sucked in a deep breath and looked at his seat mate, who grinned at him. Her lipstick-smeared teeth reminded him of a vampire ready for the second course.

"Name's Edna VanMacintosh. From Alberta, Florida."

"Uh, Brandon Morgan. Crockett County, Kentucky."

"You a coal miner or a tobacco farmer?"

"Neither, I—"

"Just kidding. I know there's also horses and hillbillies in K.Y. I'm a hairdresser," she rasped, without waiting for him to elaborate. "Was going to go on this trip with my husband for our second honeymoon, but he went and died on me."

"I'm sorry," Brandon told her after a beat. "So you're taking this trip in his memory, that's nice."

"Nah." She wheezed with laughter. "He died fifteen years ago. I was bumping uglies with his brother Si for a while, thought I might get him to come along, but then he died, too. I'm on this trip hoping to find me some new man-flesh."

"Oh." Brandon's brain froze.

She cackled and gave his ribs another jab. "Don't look so scared. You're not quite man enough for me. I like 'em a little more broken in. A few more miles on the odometer. I don't want to spend ten years trying to teach you all the tricks."

Brandon was torn between massive relief and the need to point out that in spite of the way his last few relationships had ended, he wasn't wet behind the ears.

Fortunately, massive relief won out, because Edna looked like she might be inclined to want details on his skills.

"You married? You look like the marrying kind. I bet you've got two point four kids, too."

"No, not married."

"Well, why the hell not?"

"Just haven't met the right girl, I guess." And the one he thought was "right" turned out to be terribly, horribly, wrong.

"Hmph. You a virgin?"

Brandon coughed. "Well, ma'am—"

Edna snorted. "Just kiddin'. What kind of girl you lookin' for? There's a shit ton of horny women on that cruise ship back there. I'll hook you up before we make it back to San Diego."

"I'm not really looking—"

"Are you gay? 'Cause there's plenty of single men hanging

around, too. You like the hairy ones or the twinkly kind?"

"No, no. Not gay. But I'm not looking for anyone on this cruise." He decided to elaborate, before she came up with any more wild assumptions. "Most of the girls I've met on this trip are a little too busy taking selfies and Snapchatting themselves to have a conversation."

"Oh. Well, if you're looking for a wife, you're gonna be looking for a while. You're a good-looking fella, but girls these days are all about the temporary hookup. The Redbox and Cool."

"Netflix and Chill?"

"Yeah. Whatever."

Unfortunately, Edna was right. He'd gone out with a few women in the past few years, but he always found something that didn't work for him with each one. Like…she didn't want to hang out while he added one last entry—or fifty—to a spreadsheet. Or she wanted to actually go on dates instead of visiting random liquor stores to check his company's product placement. Or maybe she'd only pretended to be crazy for him while she helped to steal thousands of dollars' worth of inventory from his family's business. Maybe he was too picky, but some of those things were deal breakers.

"I'm not looking for a wife," he told her. "But some meaningful conversation would be nice."

Edna cackled. "Is that what you kids are calling it these days?"

The bus made a hard left and lurched onto a—was this really a street? It seemed more like an alley. Trees scraped the windows on each side of the bus, before parting to reveal a boarded up house, followed by a weed-strewn yard full of broken-down cars and skinny dogs.

A hundred yards later, the bus groaned to a halt in front of a colorfully painted but rickety wooden fence, and half of the occupants immediately stood and shoved into the aisle.

Brandon waited until there was a space and stood, too. He hoped Edna would find another victim to interrogate, but alas, she actually grabbed his belt so she wouldn't lose him as he joined the milling crowd of partiers in front of the gate that read *Pequeño Zarigüeya Entrada* in colorful script.

"So what are you looking for, in case we get lucky and find you the right girl? Surgeon, lawyer, international venture capitalist?"

An international venture capitalist might be nice. They did have internet at Blue Mountain, and most of that work was on the phone or online, right? But realistically… "I don't know. Accountant? Tax attorney?" Someone who would want to climb the corporate ladder *with* him, not *over* him.

The gate opened, and a laughing, dancing, Mexican goddess swirled out into the crowd. "Welcome to the wonderful world of tequila!" she called out. "I can't wait to show you Pequeño Zarigüeya."

Okay. Maybe he should add "tequila distillery tour guide" to his list of options.

· · ·

"*Hola!*" Lesa called to the crowd of cruise goers who had gathered in front of the distillery for the day's deluxe tour and tasting.

"*Hola!*" responded the assortment of people.

Here she went again. Smile and act like you're thrilled to be here. She glanced at the sky. *Mama, I'm here, and I'm "helping."*

She didn't know if Mama would be pleased with her efforts or not, but one thing was sure—entertaining the few dozen tourists who came to Pequeño Zarigüeya each week was not going to be enough to dig Papa out of the financial hole he was in.

She did want to help the distillery survive—work was the only reason Papa got out of bed anymore. Before she died, Mama told Lesa all about how she had worked there as a girl, when her own father owned the tequileria, and was planning to go away to college until the summer Papa showed up. They had met harvesting agave, and they fell in love and got married. He'd bought Pequeño Zarigüeya from Lesa's grandfather, and they had been blissfully happy. Now Lesa must carry on. No pressure there. But more than anything, Lesa wanted the place to survive without *her*. The thought of spending yet another season trapped here made her want to scream. So she was going to sell tequila today with a smile on her face and hope in her heart that somehow, someway, they would find their way into the black.

Shifting her attention back to the crowd, Lesa got her head in the game and prepared to charm the gathered tourists—and get them to buy lots and lots of tequila. She evaluated the players. There were the dedicated drinkers, recognizable by their colorful shirts and goofy hats. Most of them already displayed half-drunken grins—and plastic cups—likely empty of their morning margaritas. These people would be good and thirsty by tasting time and it would be easy to coax them to the gift shop for a bottle or six to take back to the boat. Then there were the older couples, more sedate, but usually also ready for afternoon cocktails. They'd buy the cute little gift baskets to take home to family and friends.

There was usually a liquor snob or two, also. The liquor snob would ask dozens of questions that they already knew the answer to—or worse, jump in and answer questions from other guests before Lesa had a chance to open her mouth. At the tasting, they would swirl and breathe and make faces that said, "Meh," even though Lesa knew without a doubt that her family's tequila was the best damn booze in all of Mexico.

As for how helpful she was...Lesa really didn't think

that playing hostess to a bunch of tourists was what Papa needed right now. What he needed was a major overhaul of his business.

But this was what he asked her to do, and her English was better than the rest of the family's. Be nice to the drunks and liquor snobs alike. *Yeesh*. She was up to eight know-it-all jerks already this season, and they were only a third of the way through the spring.

Ah. There was today's know-it-all. She'd bet money on it. Tall guy in khakis and a polo shirt, bent to listen to an elderly lady with purple hair, a sports bra, and—oh, *Dios*—jeggings. Where the woman would weigh eighty pounds soaking wet, he was more substantial. Lean, but with broad shoulders and nice biceps, which he no doubt paid a personal trainer for. Medium-brown hair, a little short on the sides and longer on the top, but not too trendy. Younger than the usual jerk, but still. The deck shoes were a dead giveaway.

Okay. She knew who her crowd was, and if she was lucky, she'd be able to keep Booze Snob Guy as far away from her as possible.

Then he raised his head and laughed. And made eye contact.

Lesa forgot everything she was supposed to say to her guests.

His blue eyes held her still, and something she didn't recognize settled in her midsection. It hit him, too, because a brief expression of puzzlement crossed his face before he simply stood there, smiling at her. Her awareness of the calm warmth was quickly supplanted by the intense way her nether regions reacted to him. He was a very fine-looking Americano—as Ralph Lauren handsome as any of the California surfer boys she'd known when she'd visited Los Angeles on a rare vacation during her early college days. Nice, strong face; long, straight nose; and lips…that she'd have to check out when she got closer to him.

Not good. She never, ever messed with the tourists. She rarely even dated since coming home from college to take care of Mama during her last days.

But here she was, standing in the courtyard like a silly girl, staring at a cute boy.

The moment ended when the cougar next to him whacked him on the arm and drew his attention away.

She realized that, while she'd been falling in lust—or whatever—with the hot guy in the group, she'd been standing still, not doing her job. A whole group of guests stood staring at her, their expectation blasting through the late morning heat.

"Okay, *amigos*, here is the plan! We're going to make a quick stop in the tasting room for some tequila history, and then we'll head out to witness the way my family has made tequila for generations."

"When do we get to sample the merchandise?" one of the partiers asked.

"We'll circle back to the tasting room a few minutes before you buy everything in our gift shop." She laughed, and the audience laughed with her. A good sign.

She led the way through the courtyard of the tasting center and gift shop where her aunt held the fort. Tia Rita, Papa's youngest sister, would expertly cajole the travelers to buy anything and everything tequila, and the guests would take home tequila and memories that would keep Pequeño Zarigüeya afloat just a little longer. The memories that would—hopefully—have them buying her family's tequila and recommending it to others—if they could afford to keep making it.

Gesturing toward the open-air tasting room, she said, "Please, come in and have a seat." People filed to the long tables and sat on benches, side by side, facing her. The good-looking man chose a seat at the end of a row, about halfway back. Still not close enough to see his mouth up close.

Stop fantasizing about his lips! It wasn't like she'd ever kiss him. He'd be in her life for the next two and a half hours, and then he would be gone forever.

He saw her looking at him and smiled, sending that weird feeling to her gut again. His eyes followed her hand as she rubbed it across her tummy, trying to hold on to the sensation and categorize it. But—

"How long have you worked here?" The purple-haired woman stood in front of her, hands on hips.

"Ah…off and on since I was ten years old."

"On and off? What do you do when you're off?"

"Well…I went to college"—for almost two whole semesters—"and I like to travel." At least, she *would* like to see the world, if she didn't have to stay here and help Papa.

"Where do you travel? Who goes with you?"

Was she going to ask if she wore boxers or briefs, too? Not relevant, but she did like to personalize the tour, even if she had to stretch the truth about where she'd been into where she wanted to have been. "Everywhere I can. And mostly alone. I want to write a book about my travels on every continent on Earth."

"Are you married?"

"No." Okay, maybe not that personal. "Now, ma'am, if you'll just take your seat, we can get started."

The old lady stomped off, shaking her head. "She's a four out of ten on my suitability scale," she called back to the hot guy.

For his part, the hot guy gave her an embarrassed glance and shook his head before he looked away and helped his friend to sit next to him.

And her afternoon tour was underway.

Chapter Two

"My name ees Lesa Ruiz." Her accent was heavy, but understandable. "My papa, Carlos, his seester Tia Rita, and my cousin Raoul and I would like to welcome you to our tequileria. Pequeño Zarigüeya has been in our family for four generations."

So she was not only a tour guide, she was the owner's daughter. No wonder she was so enthusiastic. He should talk to her and find out more about Pequeño Zarigüeya. Getting close to her wouldn't be a major hardship, he mused, watching her work the crowd with her quick wit and sparkling smile, as long as he kept his head about him and didn't let her distract him from his primary purpose—to increase Blue Mountain Bourbon's profits.

"What's a peeking zeriquaya?" Edna asked. "Some kind of lizard?"

Lesa Ruiz lit up the already bright room with her smile. "Pequeño Zarigüeya means 'little opossum.' The story goes that when my great-great-grandfather started making tequila here many years ago, there was a family of opossum living in the rafters of the room where we stored the agave. They would steal them occasionally, and supposedly he found the whole family drunk from an agave that had begun to ferment before it was even cooked and mashed."

"Well, that's just cute, now, isn't it?" Some big guy on the other side of the room commented.

Asshole.

Lesa ignored him and went on. "I want to know where are your homes," she told the assembled group. "Let's start over here."

The big man in the floral shirt told her that he was a dentist and his group was from Houston, Texas. There was an older couple from Florida, and another from Nebraska, both retired. Several couples were from Canada.

There was Edna, from Florida.

"I'm Brandon Morgan, from Crockett County, Kentucky."

"What ees your job in Kentucky?" Lesa asked.

"Marketing."

She tilted her head. "You buy the groceries?"

Huh? "Well, sometimes, when my mom can't take my grandma."

She smiled at him, then spoke slowly, to make him understand. "But what is your job."

"Marketing."

"You buy groceries for your family? That is your job?"

Oh. *Marketing.* She thought—

The giant flower-covered dentist guffawed, and Brandon thought about headbutting him.

Instead, he smiled, and said, "Yes. And I work at our family's business."

"What do you do for your family's business?" She was determined to get to the bottom of his life, wasn't she? Brandon felt absurdly pleased that she was so interested.

"I oversee advertising and broker sales contracts with

distributors."

"Oh!" She threw her head back, the music of her laughter ringing a chime in Brandon. "You're in *marketing*."

"Well, yes. For my company, and occasionally for my family."

Their eyes met, and for one long second, Brandon forgot every rule he'd made about not getting involved with anyone in the booze business ever again.

"Don't even think about it," Edna hissed. "She's not your type."

The moment broken, Lesa returned her attention to the group. "Let me tell you a little bit about tequila."

Brandon found himself captivated, not only by Lesa, but by her presentation of the history of tequila production. Her clever stories—and the beguiling smiles she sent his way—almost made him want to drink the stuff. Almost.

Some of what she said was information he already knew. Just as all bourbons are whiskey, but not all whiskies are bourbons, all tequilas are mescal—distilled from a fermented agave plant— but not all mescals are tequila. And just as bourbon had to be at least 51% corn, tequila had to be at least 51% agave.

But there was other information that he'd never heard, or never paid much attention to, because he didn't like tequila. After all, his family made the best bourbon in Kentucky. Though if he were to follow through on his plans, he should probably be willing to find out more.

As everyone filed from the room toward the production facilities, she shared stories of ancient Aztecs and Spanish conquerors, family businesses and family feuds. Brandon appreciated that this wasn't a canned introduction, like in so many other tours he'd been on—from distilleries to Disney—though he knew this one would end in a gift shop, just like the Small World ride. His family was working on building a similar end to the Blue Mountain tour, so he got it.

He was almost distracted enough by her stories to miss the signs that Pequeño Zarigüeya was a struggling enterprise. It wasn't the worn equipment—it all appeared to be in good working order in spite of the age of some of the machines. It was more the discrepancies in inventory. Too many empty bottles, not enough full barrels of aging product. An advertising campaign that was horribly outdated. Things like that. The little possum needed a new direction.

The guide obviously not only knew her stuff, but she believed in it. It was too bad she wasn't passionate about bourbon. Blue Mountain could use someone like her.

Someone who, as Edna had so generously pointed out, wasn't his type. She was bubbly and outgoing and interested in travel. He was solid, occasionally introverted, and a dedicated homebody.

The group was led back across a nice little courtyard with a fountain and a couple of benches.

"Couldn't you just live here forever?" sighed Edna, looking up at a colorful bird perched on the wall surrounding the courtyard.

"Naw. I'm a Kentucky boy through and through."

The dentist turned with a smirk. "Seriously? What's so great about the Bluegrass?"

Everyone was looking at him. Brandon already didn't like Dr. Smug for laughing at Lesa's misunderstanding of his job. But he was a grown-up, and wouldn't challenge him to a duel. He would take the high road. Besides, he was a lousy shot.

"If you've never been there, Kentucky's the most beautiful state in the world. We've got rolling hills with miles of white fences and thoroughbred racehorses, and other parts have mountains and valleys with rock formations you wouldn't believe. Some of the best lakes for boating and fishing you can imagine. Oh. And forests for camping and hunting and hiking. There are miles and miles of limestone caves made by underground rivers. And last but not least, the best damned bourbon in the universe, which is made by my family, at the Blue Mountain Distillery."

The crowd had grown silent, staring at him. Lesa had her head tilted to the side, eyes wide.

Okay, maybe that was a little too much. "So anyway, that's where I'm from."

"If Kentucky's so damned fabulous, what are you doing on this cruise?" someone muttered, loud enough for everyone to hear.

He scratched his chin. "I needed a quiet stateroom to get some work done."

. . .

After seeing the kilns where the agave was roasted before fermenting, the stills where the alcohol was boiled away from the mash, the warehouse where liquor was aged, and the bottling facility, Brandon was more interested in tequila than he thought he would ever be. And an idea he'd had before he'd come on this trip was starting to take on a life of its own. He was going to have to have a conversation with Señorita Ruiz.

"And now we have come to the most popular part of the visit…the samples!"

The crowd cheered and rushed for the tasting room. Unlike the first time they'd been in this room, everyone settled down immediately, waiting for Lesa to start her spiel about the different types of tequila her company produced.

A young man, who Lesa had introduced earlier as her cousin, began passing out small wooden trays, each with five tiny shot glasses. Each little plastic cup held a splash of liquid, ranging in color from clear to pale gold to amber.

When the kid got to Brandon, he almost waved the tray away. He looked up to see Lesa watching him with suspicion. What had he done? He'd asked a few questions on the tour, but nothing that would make her think he was going to spit in her booze. In the end, he thanked his server and took the tray.

Edna immediately picked up the darkest liquor on her own tray and threw it back, smacking her lips with gusto. "Damn. That's some fine shit," she said, pounding her chest.

"I think you're supposed to wait until she talks about each type, so you can appreciate the flavors," Brandon whispered.

"Hah. I'm not drinking it for the taste." She picked up the next cup. "I'm working up my courage to go talk to that guy over there." She indicated an older gentleman sitting with a plump, smiling woman about the same age. Brandon thought they were the couple who was also from Florida.

"Edna, I think he's married to the lady he's holding hands with."

"Eh, no biggie." She waved her hand in dismissal. "She told me in the bathroom that she's got a heart condition. I'll make friends with him now, and he'll be single by the time I get back to Alberta and put my house up for sale."

Brandon was left speechless, but was saved from having to respond by Lesa, who cleared her throat and announced, "Okay. Now that everyone's been served, we can begin. I want you to pick up the medium colored tequila, and bring it to your nose." She held up her own cup. "This is Pequeño Zarigüeya Gold, which is our most popular tequila for margaritas."

Brandon dutifully sniffed each cup, and worked to appreciate the flavor notes that she described. It really didn't smell as horrible as his memory would have him believe. He was actually able to appreciate the sweet herbal aroma, but he still slid each cup to Edna instead of drinking it himself.

He didn't need to drink it, though, to have ideas—it was the aging process that was of greatest interest to Brandon.

There were some definite implications for both Blue Mountain Bourbon and Pequeño Zarigüeya Distilling, if he wasn't mistaken.

"You have just tasted our Reposado Especial—Special Reserve," Lesa announced after the next sample, and with a dramatic pause, added, "The liquor we only share with our premium tour guests. Aged in French oak barrels for at least three years, it is our finest tequila. This last tequila is our least expensive. It has more of a bite, but I saved it for last because I wanted you to see how different—and yet how similar—it is to our Special Reserve."

She'd been strolling through the crowd as she spoke, but hadn't paused. This time she did. Standing right in front of Brandon, she looked down at him and put a hand on her hip. Her curvy, luscious hip. Staring straight at Brandon, she pointed at the clear liquid remaining in front of him and said, "Now taste."

She had totally noticed that he wasn't drinking.

Ah, hell.

• • •

Brandon from Kentucky wasn't drinking her tequila, and Lesa really wanted him to like it. She wanted everyone to like it, of course, but for some reason, it was important that he appreciate what she had to offer. In terms of tequila, of course. The way he met her eyes when he smiled had nothing at all to do with it.

Maybe it was because Mr. Sexy was not only a liquor snob, he was another distiller. Was he here to look down his nose at her? She discarded that idea. He was too cute and friendly. Although…maybe he was here to rescue Pequeño Zarigüeya and just didn't know it yet? She had to get him to drink.

"Ahm not much of a tequila drinker," he drawled.

"Well, *y'all* should give it a try."

The eye-contact-smile thing happened again. "Are y'all makin' fun of the way I talk?"

"Ahm tryin' to," she told him.

"Ahm not sure you're going to get any awards from the Southern Accent Society of America, but there's hope. *Y'all* should probably spend some time immersed in the culture before you try out for the team."

She giggled, but didn't offer to immerse herself in *his* culture, as much as the thought appealed to her.

He sure seemed to believe his travel-guide hype. This guy genuinely loved his home. Listening to him made her consider a visit to Kentucky on her "Places to go as soon as I get a chance" tour.

She'd never considered Middle America somewhere interesting. But here was this guy...this...love child of a moonshiner and a Derby horse owner, and she was starting to think...*stuff*...about Mr. Booze Snob.

She didn't find him as snooty as she'd expected. He'd asked questions on the tour, but they'd been insightful and challenging in an interesting way. He hadn't been know-it-allish about liquor, and the only time he'd answered a question addressed to her was when someone asked about whiskey, which she knew little about.

Lesa had read travel articles about places all over the world, and sampled potent potables from Bordeaux, France, to Kamchatka, Russia. But not Kentucky, and not bourbon. The Scotch whiskey she'd tried hadn't done much for her, and she couldn't imagine that scotch's younger brother from America could taste any better.

The travel jones had been strong lately. Maybe her attraction to this Brandon was transference: wanderlust subverted to man-lust. No time for that, though. She had to help Papa get Pequeño Zarigüeya on its feet so she could go live her life elsewhere.

"Ahm a-waitin'," she reminded him, drawing a laugh from those sitting nearby.

He hesitated. Took a deep sniff of the tequila. Shrugged, raised his cup to her, and let half the liquid inside slip over his bottom lip. His eyes narrowed in consideration. He tilted his head back and forth, still tasting. Then finally, a swallow. "Huh. That didn't suck."

She laughed.

He smiled ruefully, one chunk of light brown hair flopping over his forehead in a disarmingly attractive manner. "Sorry. Bad experience with tequila in college. I've been avoiding it ever since."

"Well then, you must have been drinking bad tequila."

He nodded, tipped the rest of the liquor into his fine mouth and said, "I might have to agree with you."

"Well, I'm glad to have changed your opinion." *What's your opinion of me?* She wouldn't ask that, of course. She was just another tour guide on a rich bourbon boy's cruise itinerary. He was just another tourist. Except he wasn't. No other visitor in recent—in any—memory gave her funny feelings in her tummy.

"Excuse me. Are we done here?" It was one of the big drinkers, a giant, red-faced man with a hot pink Tommy Bahama shirt over a pair of black-and-white checkered board shorts.

"Oh!" She turned away from Distraction Man. She'd completely forgotten her job. "Yes. Thank you, ladies and gentlemen, for coming to visit us here and to enjoy our fine tequila! Feel free to wander through the courtyard and visit our little store if you're inclined. I'll come to wish you all good-bye before your bus returns you to Puerto Vallarta."

Lesa turned back to see that Brandon was helping his friend Edna to her feet. She liked that he had befriended an old person that way. Unfortunately for her, it looked like he'd be occupied for the next few minutes, because Edna was wasted.

"Hey, let me go, Captain Hottypants." Edna slapped at Brandon's arm, laughing—or maybe wheezing. "Just because you gave me a bunch of drinks doesn't give you the right to manhandle me."

Brandon released her like a hot tamale. She scuttled away and clamped on to a man and woman her own age. "Hey, I want to talk to you two about some future plans. Let's go to the courtyard and find a seat."

And suddenly Lesa was alone with Brandon. She was the woman who never had trouble talking to anyone, from anywhere, about anything, but she was suddenly struck mute.

She couldn't stop looking at him long enough to think of anything to say. Those blue eyes, and the short brown hair with the funny cowlick. The almost too big nose. His lips were soft. The bottom one was the tiniest bit biteable, and the top looked firm and had a perfect divot in the middle, except for the little scar on the left side.

The quiet that flooded the newly emptied room gathered between them.

Rolling her eyes, she mentally slapped herself in the head. "So. You didn't like tequila, but now you like it again. I have done my job. But if you didn't like it in the first place, why did you come today?"

He smiled crookedly. "To avoid death by fun."

"What does that mean?"

He shrugged. "Never mind. I'm glad I came, because I happen to have something that just might give your next casking of Special Reserve some new life."

Lesa was speechless again, but not because she was in the crush zone.

"What's wrong?"

"Nothing." *Except maybe you're the answer to my prayers?*

"So what is your idea?"

"You're currently using French oak barrels for your Special Reserve, right?"

"Yes…" At least, they had been. Before the past two years of bad weather had wrecked the agave harvest, and their barrel importer was threatening to give their contract to another company. Yet another thread in the fragile rope holding Pequeño Zarigüeya above Lesa's head waiting to crush her hopes and dreams of escape.

"And if your young tequila doesn't suck, then your Special Reserve is probably okay."

"Well, I might go a step beyond that."

His acquiescent smile made her want to touch that little scar on his lip. With her tongue.

"But what if you used a different kind of barrel? One that would meld the smoky-sweet Blue Mountain magic with your tequila, and make it into something that would get awards and orders from the finest establishments in the world?"

Lesa was already interested in anything that rolled off this almost-country-boy's tongue, but if he had an idea that might pull Pequeño Zarigüeya out of the red? Now she was *very* interested.

Chapter Three

Brandon threw the idea out to Lesa. "I think you should try aging your tequila in used Blue Mountain bourbon barrels. Giving your new tequila a few months in our oak is going to make it amazing."

The idea had been meandering around in his head before he'd even gotten here. Bourbon was the hottest drink around these days, but trends changed, and there was always room for one more hip liquor. Just like the stock market, diversifying their holdings was a good idea. He'd talked to the board of Blue Mountain—his father and his neighbor Lorena McGrath—about searching for new business partners. This might be the right thing.

So he explained his idea to Lesa. Bourbon barrels, as a rule, were always built of new oak. But after they'd been used once, they were sold and repurposed, often by other distillers to age scotch, wine, *tequila*… There was also a very popular brand of beer that was held in bourbon barrels.

Lesa had made a big deal about the costly French oak barrels they used for their Reposado, but after a quick Google search on his phone, Brandon's opinion was that the barrels were overpriced, especially for the flavor they imparted. He could get Lesa's family a much better deal, and it looked like they could use a good deal right now. He'd have to do some fancy dancing, if they were interested, because he had to make a contract decision about selling barrels to their regular wholesale buyer soon, but if it worked out, the deal would benefit both distilleries in a potentially big way.

Lesa was listening and nodding her head. She tucked a strand of dark hair behind her ear.

"You look skeptical."

"Well," she said, a charming blush staining her cheeks.

"What?" He kicked the toe of her sneaker gently. When had he gotten so close to her? He caught a whiff of orange and lime, as though she were a human margarita. Would she taste like that…tangy, and salty, and sweet?

He needed to back away from the temptation to find out. He was making a business proposal, not asking her out on a date. As he well knew, mixing the two was a bad idea. "Come on, what do you have against bourbon barrels? Is it because you're thinking of a barefoot guy with a long beard, a shotgun across his knee, guarding a still?"

She laughed. "No. I um…I don't like whiskey."

"Well, well, well. You know what? I don't like tequila, either."

She pushed at his shoulder. "I don't not like it because I have hangover, ah, what's the word? *Flashbacks*," she teased. "I went to a scotch whiskey tasting a few years ago, and each version was worse than the last!"

He understood. "You had scotch, not bourbon."

"But it's all whiskey," she argued. "And it's like eating— drinking—burning dirt."

"Wow. That's…descriptive. And wrong. Bourbon is a lot different from scotch. Yes, they're both liquor distilled from grain. But bourbon has a higher percentage of corn, and it's sweeter. Maybe you should give it a try before you dismiss it out of hand."

"Really? Too bad we don't have any here for me to taste." She raised an eyebrow and looked him over.

He felt her eyes roam over his shirt, his pants. He stepped back, worried that her warm, coffee gaze would heat him up too much. Besides, he was talking her into trying bourbon, not him. "As a matter of fact, I do." He swung his pack up and pulled at the drawstring. "You're going to have to put your pesos where your mouth is, señorita."

"Oh boy."

He could tell that she knew when she was beat. He'd been a good sport about the tequila, she'd have to give his liquor a try. As he pulled the bottle free and worked at the seal, Lesa got a couple of glasses and sat sideways on the nearest bench. Brandon straddled the other end of the bench, facing her, and pulled a glass closer.

Tipping the bottle, they watched the amber liquid splash against the bottom of the glass until there was an inch or so inside.

Then he pushed it toward her. "Some people like a little ice, a little water, but if you're really gonna taste it, then room temperature is best."

Lesa nodded and carefully picked up the glass. She leaned over, holding it as far from her body as possible, and delicately sniffed.

"It's not gonna bite you."

She looked up at him, raising an eyebrow. "Are you sure?"

He couldn't quite answer, because her position had given him a distracting view—right down the front of her blouse. Fortunately he caught himself before she did, and turned to pull the other glass closer.

"Oh no you don't," she said as he began to pour bourbon

for himself. "You have to try the Special Reserve."

He looked at her, and the way she held his family's pride and joy within kissing distance.

"Fine." He grabbed the nearby bottle of tequila and filled his own glass.

"Ready?" she asked.

"Ready."

They both took small sips, holding each other's gaze. Brandon wasn't sure if it was the alcohol or the dark heat in her eyes that made him dizzy, but he found himself swallowing the entire contents of the glass.

It really was pretty good. He detected the oak—that was as familiar to him as the scent of pine trees in the winter. But he was even more certain that using Blue Mountain barrels would make this liquor even better.

She shot the remaining contents in one swallow, *thunk*ing her empty glass on the table. "This doesn't taste as much like horse pee as I expected," she gasped.

Aaaand she was refilling their glasses, and he was drinking again.

"So you're the heir to Blue Mountain Bourbon."

"One of them. There are five—er, four of us. Kids of the current two families who own the business."

"Five, or four?"

"Oh. Well, there were five of us, but David McGrath, the son of the other family, he was a marine and died in the Middle East."

"Oh. I'm sorry." She touched his leg in sympathy. Though she removed it quickly, the heat trail from her fingers traced up his thigh.

"Thanks. We miss him."

She brought the topic back on safer ground. "And where are you in line for the throne?"

Brandon snorted. "It's not like that. We each get a fourth.

But I'm oldest."

"And is Brandon a family name?" Lesa sipped the bourbon, watching him closely.

"Nope. But my middle name, Frank, is the same as my dad's and grandfather's."

"Brandon Frank Morgan." She nodded. "Very…"

"Boring?"

Her smile grew teasing, sending tendrils of arousal along with the liquor invading his blood. "Ees Brrandon Frrank Morgan a dull boy?" Her accent was thickening in response to her rising blood alcohol level. And it was really freaking sexy.

He cleared his throat. "It depends on your definition of dull." Where was this going? He looked at the woman across from him and wanted to know what the taste of tequila in his own mouth would be like mixed with bourbon in hers.

He couldn't do this. He was supposed to be working. Wasn't he? "So what do you do besides leading tours here?" Brandon asked. He found he wanted to know more about this woman with the saucy smile and the apparent ability to keep up with him at the bar.

"Not much right now, but I aspire to be a professional gypsy," she told him, taking another, slower sip of bourbon.

"What, exactly, does that mean?"

"I want to travel, to write about traveling, and then travel some more."

"So you don't want to stay here and run the business?"

She shuddered, but Brandon wasn't sure if it was because of the gulp of whiskey she'd just swallowed, or because the idea of being a full-time distillery employee was abhorrent to her. That would be a shame. Brandon couldn't think of anything he loved more than his work.

"No. I…I've put in my time here. I want to come only occasionally to visit."

"Your parents would miss you, wouldn't they?"

She nodded. "Yeah. Papa would prefer that I stay, but I—" She shook her head. "And my mother died a few years ago."

"That's too bad. Your father hasn't remarried?"

She snorted. "He never leaves the distillery to meet anyone new."

She didn't elaborate, so Brandon didn't push, but he sensed there was more to the story.

Quite the seducer, he was, bringing up sad stuff again.

But she didn't seem to be too bothered. She took another sip of her drink and said, "So. You want us to put a season's worth of Special Reserve into your barrels."

Oh yeah. He was here to talk business, not autobiographies. But for the life of him, he couldn't remember what his terms should be.

Looking at her, he took another sip. And then another. She was right in front of him now. The warmth of her body next to him was as intoxicating as the liquor. Bending his head toward her, he lowered his mouth. Her face tilted up to his. He was going to kiss her. And she was going to let him.

He—

"Lesa!"

They jumped apart from each other as an elderly woman, spewing rapid Spanish, came toward them. She asked a question, and Lesa put her hand over her mouth, but not before Brandon was able to translate the curse words she tried to muffle.

The older woman threw up her hands and said something else, which had Lesa shaking her head and frowning. Then the woman—Tia Rita?—patted her on the arm and turned to go back toward the door. She looked at Brandon and shook her finger at him with a grin. He didn't know what she said, but understood the universal language of "you're a bad, bad boy."

"What's wrong?" Brandon asked, as Lesa sat down on

the table, staring at him with a guilty smile.

"Well, I made you miss your bus."

"Oh, shit!" He started to move toward the door.

"Don't bother. They're long gone."

He couldn't believe that he'd spent so much time flirting with her. A quick glance at his watch told him that he'd have to find a cab quickly to get him back to the shuttle boat in time to get back on the cruise ship. "Any chance there's a cab company anywhere close by?"

She shook her head. "No. But I'll take you. Or rather, I'll get my cousin Raoul to drive you, and I will come, too. I want to get some things in town and it will save me a trip tomorrow"

As much as the thought of spending another couple of hours in her company appealed to him, he couldn't ask her to do that. "You won't get back here until late, and you've got tours to give in the morning, don't you?"

"Actually, no I don't. We're closing for tours for the next few weeks because they are going to be replacing parts of the road to the city."

"Oh. Well." Suddenly his missed bus had turned into good luck. "In that case, my only regret about missing the bus is that the boat will be leaving, and I won't have time to buy you dinner when we get back to town."

"That is a shame." And she did look disappointed. She stood, swaying for a brief second. "Come to the house with me, Brank Morgan. I mean, Brankon Frand. I mean—never mind. Come with me and I'll get Raoul. You can meet my father and tell him your idea."

• • •

Lesa's head began to clear as she led Brandon into her father's house. He had clouded her senses—and not just with the booze. He was sooo cute.

As she held the door for Brandon, she hoped Papa had gotten dressed since she'd left him there this morning. The past couple of years had been hard on him. He'd been gone most of the time when she was younger—while Mama was sick, which was from as far back as she could remember until she died just a few years ago. Papa worked constantly, never home for Mama because he was trying to earn money to pay for a cure. Which hadn't worked. And now the driven distiller of her childhood had been replaced by a bitter, grieving shadow— though he'd functioned. Then two years of bad harvests had put Pequeño Zarigüeya in the red. The difficulty had flipped a switch, and for a while, it seemed like he was back to his old workaholic self. But it was an up and down thing. Some days he worked with a desperation that frightened her. Other days, he seemed to have given up. Maybe this new barrel idea would drag him out of his current slump. He could get Pequeño Zarigüeya back on its feet, and she could leave with a clear conscience.

"Papa?" she called, as Brandon followed her from the entryway down the hall.

Watching television. Again.

Papa was in his small, dark living area, where blue light reflected over the small man in his recliner. The house smelled of spices and despair, and the familiar claustrophobia Lesa felt in here reached out with its claws. There was a beautiful mountain vista just beyond the darkened curtains. Why didn't Papa ever open the windows and let some fresh air and light in?

It was a rhetorical complaint, so she didn't voice it.

"*Hola*, Lesa," Papa said, looking away from the TV for a moment. He started to return his attention to his show, but then did a double take, sitting up and putting the remote aside. "Who is your guest?"

"*Hola*, Papa. This is Brandon Morgan, from Kentucky in America. His tour bus left without him because we were talking about business."

And maybe almost kissing. He had been about to kiss her, hadn't he?

Papa jerked the recliner into an upright position and stood, a wide, bright smile spreading across his old face. He held out his hand for Brandon to shake. "Brandon Morgan. From Blue Mountain?"

"Yes, sir," Brandon answered. "You know of Blue Mountain Bourbon, then."

"Oh, yes. I have had many occasions to taste your family's product. It's fine quality."

When she snorted, both men turned to look at Lesa. "Sorry. Some, ah, dust in my nose."

Brandon grinned. She didn't have him fooled. She'd liked his whiskey, in spite of herself.

She waved at the men. "Go ahead. Tell him your idea. Papa, may I borrow the car keys?"

"Where are you going?" Papa's brow furrowed.

"Brandon missed his tour bus, and he'll miss his cruise ship if we don't catch them in Puerto Vallarta. If it's all right with you, I'll get Raoul and we'll drive him to the city."

"That is fine." She listened to Brandon's pitch as she dug through the mess on the end table for Papa's keys. He rarely went anywhere, but still insisted on keeping his keys within arm's reach at all times, wanting everyone to ask his permission to drive. Another weird quirk that chafed.

Brandon explained the concept of aging tequila in used bourbon barrels, melding the exclusive qualities of both distilleries into a final product that would be exponentially better than it would be when aged in a run-of-the-mill barrel.

Papa listened politely, but then said, "I don't know. Even if this makes the best tequila in the universe, I have heard rumors about your company. There was a fire there, just last week, if I'm not mistaken. How do I know, if I buy your barrels, that you won't have another fire, or some other catastrophe, and then I will be, how do you say it? Screwed."

"Sir, you have my word that we are solid. The fire in our rickhouse was a human error that won't be repeated."

"You have disowned your brother?"

Lesa listened to the interchange with surprise. For someone who barely left the house, Papa knew things Lesa would never have guessed. So just what had happened at Blue Mountain Bourbon?

As though reading her mind, Brandon turned to explain, "My brother Justin accidentally caught our newest aging warehouse on fire. Fortunately, the rickhouse had been nearly empty, and no stock was lost. It's all good. Well. With the exception of making the 'Happenings' section in the Distilled Spirits Weekly blog." To her father, he said, "No, sir, my brother is still part of the family. Accidents happen, and he is, more than anyone else, determined that nothing like this will ever happen again."

Papa harrumphed.

"You're welcome to come visit and see for yourself. Talk to my family and the McGraths, who are co-owners."

Eyes narrowed, Papa pointed at Brandon. "And there was that business several years ago with the other family. The McGrath man."

Brandon sighed. "I can assure you, sir. Since I took over Jamie's position, we are in sound financial shape."

"No problems with, say, theft or embezzlement?"

At this, Brandon's shoulders stiffened. Through tight lips, he ground out, "We're in good shape, sir."

"I don't really believe this is a good idea."

The air blew right out of Lesa's sails. Right through the living room and down the side of the mountain.

"Papa, I really think this *is* a good idea. We should check it out."

Brandon looked from Papa to Lesa. "Like I said. You're welcome to visit any time."

Maybe this was just what Papa needed to get over his depression. A trip to Kentucky.

"No. I don't think so."

"Can I talk to you?" Lesa tugged him toward the kitchen. "We'll be right back," she told Brandon.

When they were alone, Papa said, arms crossed over his chest, "I don't trust him."

"Why not?"

"He wants to take advantage of us. He's too shiny. Too perfect. An answer for everything."

Lesa almost pointed out that Brandon's hair kept falling over his forehead, but didn't think that's what Papa meant. And her gut told her that this was a good plan.

"You should go to Kentucky, since he invited you," Lesa suggested. "You need a vacation anyway."

"I don't vacation. Holidays are for the weak."

Lesa's eye began to twitch, and she blinked to keep Papa from noticing. It was the same argument they'd had forever, and yet it always stressed her out.

Papa's eyes sharpened. "I know. You will go with him and find out if this place is okay," Papa said.

"What?" Her heart leaped, but she wasn't sure she'd heard him right. Papa never wanted her to do anything but greet tourists and file paperwork.

"We're going to be closed to tourists for a while. You don't have anything else to do. I do. I have meetings with suppliers all week." Probably to bargain for more time to pay the bills. "You will see if this Blue Mountain Distillery is as safe and stable as Mr. Morgan says it is. You'll report back to me, and then we will decide about making a deal." He nodded as though this was a done deal.

Lesa wasn't about to argue. He probably thought that if she got to take a short vacation to the U.S., her dreams of leaving the tequileria to travel the world would be satisfied, and she wasn't going to tell him there was nothing in the universe that would stop her from leaving Pequeño Zarigüeya–leaving Mexico altogether—for good, as soon as she had a chance.

He turned and went back to the living room and said to Brandon, "Lesa will come with you. This is okay?"

Brandon shot her a look that was part pleasant surprise and part deer in the headlights.

"Well, sure." He shrugged those wide shoulders.

"But remember *jefe*—you touch my daughter? You die."

Brandon's shoulders got a little broader, his straight back a little more rigid. *Dios*, he was *bueno*.

"Sir, I would never do anything Lesa didn't want me to do." The determined way he didn't look at her spoke volumes. Volumes Lesa was willing to fill with exquisite details about what she might like him to do to her.

"That's not exactly what I said," Papa told him, but after a moment of steely eyed intimidation, waved him off.

She sent a quick prayer of rationalization to heaven. *Mama? This counts as helping Papa, right?* Funny how fast the answer came back to her.

Before Papa could change his mind, Lesa took off down the hall and said, "I'll pack." She touched her fingertips to Mama's picture, where it hung in the hallway next to Jesus, between her and Papa's bedrooms. She figured Mama would approve—after all, some of her last words, before the cancer killed her, were "Follow your dreams and help your Papa keep Pequeño Zarigüeya alive." Considering that her dream was to travel, not to slave away at the struggling tequileria for the rest of her life, this was the best of both worlds.

Papa followed her into her room. As she tugged the

ancient suitcase from beneath the bed, he said, "You think this is a good chance for us?"

"Yes, I think so," she told him, with a kiss to the cheek. She grabbed three pairs of sandals and tossed them in the suitcase. The new gold heels might finally get a workout. "If you do this deal with Blue Mountain, and they help us with promoting the tequila, we'll be in good shape in no time."

Papa shook his gray head. "Maybe, but I need you to be sure."

Lesa narrowed her eyes, folding a dress and laying it over her favorite jeans. "Okay, Papa. I'll keep my eyes open."

He shook his head. "You will do more than keep your eyes open. You will look. Do you understand? Make sure there is nothing risky going on there."

"You want me to spy?"

"It's not spying. It's business. He would do the same thing. He may even be doing his own corporate espionage as we speak."

Lesa stuck her head out of her bedroom door and looked down the hall. Brandon stood with his hands in his pockets, examining the hundreds of family photos on the wall behind the couch. When he noticed her in his peripheral vision, he turned his head and smiled at her, an open, honest smile. *Oh, that smile.* And she was going to get to bask in it for a bit.

"Okay," she told Papa.

"You're a good girl," Papa repeated. "Your mama would be proud of you."

She hoped so, she really did.

Chapter Four

Brandon maneuvered his old SUV up the long, winding driveway to his family home, glancing over at the sleeping Lesa. He wondered at her ability to sack out so completely. She'd barely murmured when he swerved to avoid hitting a deer that jumped in front of the car a few miles earlier.

How on earth had he managed to pick up a girl on vacation and bring her home with him? He imagined his bus riding partner Edna giving a thumbs up, but his sadder, wiser conscience warned him that he might be making a terrible mistake. She was a woman, and he was…weak. No, scratch that. He'd been weak once. Not anymore. He'd learned from his mistake—from Suzanne—and he wasn't going to be blinded by a pretty face—and sexy body—ever again.

But damn. If he was going to have a fling with a business associate ever again…nope. No fling, no matter how much his body was trying to remind him that he was still on vacation.

He shifted in his seat. His pants had been too tight since he'd met this woman. He had a brief moment of panic—what was he doing? Had his arousal-clouded mind influenced his decision to propose a barrel deal with Pequeño Zarigüeya? And what about his larger goal? To increase the reach of Blue Mountain Distilling into other markets? He had a fantasy that someday his family would have a hand in every pot—or still–in the world. Tequila now, then Scotch. Russian vodka. German—well, beer. That wouldn't require a still. But he had to keep his mind on the long-term goal and not get distracted by sex.

Though her father *had* threatened to kill him. Which tweaked the testosterone-fueled section of his—he-man brain?–well, whichever brain that was. But no, that wasn't what attracted him to her. It was her quick wit, her easy smile, her energy and enthusiasm.

Lesa was here to evaluate the distillery for its financial stability. Not to get busy with the owner's son during the time they'd be spending together. Closely together.

Everything had become a complete whirlwind once it had been decided that she'd come with him to visit the distillery. Brandon called his parents and grandparents, who were still on the cruise ship, to let them know of his plans. He was still a little embarrassed at how loudly Gramps had cackled over the line. "Boy, you don't just get lucky, do you? You win the damned lottery!" Lesa had heard him—how could she not?—and given a tiny, almost secret, smile.

After he let the cruise company know he wouldn't be returning—and wasn't lost at sea—they'd made plane reservations and rushed to the airport to make the last flight of the day. Lesa's cousin had driven them, and he chattered the whole time, practicing his English.

The cousin was especially interested to learn which celebrities Brandon knew. After assuring Raoul that he didn't know Tom Hiddleston, Brad Pitt, or even Vin Diesel, the boy moved on to hip-hop stars, most of whom Brandon hadn't even heard of. He was afraid he was a terrible disappointment, but Lesa assured him that Raoul told her that he thought Brandon was the shit.

They hadn't been able to get seats next to each other on the plane, and she'd fallen asleep moments after they got into the car.

"Hey, Lesa. Lesa, we're here." He put the vehicle into park and gently shook her shoulder.

"Oh." She pushed her silky, black hair away from her face and smiled sleepily. A surge of affection and lust shot through him. He wouldn't mind seeing that drowsy expression first thing in the morning. On the pillow next to his.

"I hope there's an unoccupied sofa available. I think I'm going to sink into it and stay there until noon tomorrow."

"Yes. Absolutely. Except there are empty beds. Mine. I mean…you can have my bed, and I'll sleep in my brother's room." Good reminder that she wasn't here to sleep with him. At all. She was a business associate. And pillow sharing wasn't included in any of Blue Mountain Bourbon's contracts.

She stifled a yawn and said, "I won't argue tonight. I'm too tired—but I don't want to put you out of your own bed."

As they exited the car and gathered Lesa's things—Brandon's bags were still on the cruise ship and would come home with his parents—the chilly Kentucky spring wind blew the scent of home into his lungs.

Breathing deep, he sighed. "Just smell that air."

Lesa sniffed, wrinkling her nose. "Huh."

"Doesn't it smell great? New grass, the woods just starting to come back to life?"

She smiled at him, and he realized he must sound like a complete dweeb.

He shrugged, embarrassed. "Sorry. I just love this place."

"I can see that." She looked wistful, turning to peer down the hill. On one side of the drive, over a rise at the bottom, was the distillery. Security lights on poles shone a fuzzy, yellow glow in the misty midnight air.

"So that's it," she observed.

"Yeah." He tried to see it from a stranger's point of view.

A cluster of buildings of odd shapes and sizes all connected by cobblestone paths. Over the hill, he knew, was the building site for the new visitor's center and tasting room. Farther away were the rickhouses. First the old one, tall, narrow, and weathered from the years and years of sun and rain. Tiny windows pierced the sides to allow airflow inside the warehouse, making it look like a prison, or a sweatshop factory, he supposed.

Beyond that was the newer storage facility, shaped the same, but daylight would show its more uniform coloring because it hadn't suffered as much abuse. Well, except for the fire damage. He'd only seen photos that his brother had sent after the fire. Hopefully the new construction would be underway soon.

Sooner than soon, actually, if he was to convince Lesa that everything at Blue Mountain was copacetic.

Lesa tugged at the backpack Brandon held for her, and he let her have it, hoisting the heavier duffel over his shoulder and shutting the back end of his vehicle.

A security light illuminated the long stairway to the deck that led into the kitchen...the only entrance anyone here used. There was a front door, but it overlooked the other side of the hill, toward the main road, so only people driving by ever saw it. Mom said it was dumb to have even built a front door.

"Hang on," he said, before they went up the steps. He bent over and picked up the solar-powered glow-in-the-dark frog at the bottom of the steps. Yep, there it was, the same house key they'd been using since he and his brother were old enough to be out without their parents. "Okay. Let's get inside and get you settled in for the night."

Yawning, she said, "That sounds wonderful. I can't wait to get up tomorrow and see everything there is to see about this Kentucky you are so proud of. And Blue Mountain Bourbon."

God, he'd love to show her around Kentucky. Too bad they'd be spending all of their time together going over the books and the facilities with a fine-toothed comb.

That was a weird thought. While he did love his state, and had waxed nostalgic over it just a few hours ago, he hadn't done any local stuff in years, preferring to work, rather than waste time having fun. Although he was supposed to still be on vacation with his family. Maybe they could find a little time to sightsee. The thought didn't give him as many heebie-jeebies as he expected.

He climbed the stairs behind Lesa. And her behind, which swayed with every step she took. Hypnotized, he nearly stumbled into her when she reached the top and halted.

"You okay?" she asked.

"I, uh, think maybe I'm more tired than I realized," he lied.

"Well, then, good night, Brank," she said with a wink, reminding him of the kiss they'd almost shared in the tequileria.

Ah, hell. He was going to be lying awake for a long time tonight, thinking about the warm woman sleeping in his bed.

• • •

Lesa slid between the clean, crisp sheets on Brandon's bed and breathed in his scent. The room was steeped in him. He—and his room—smelled...good. Honest. Like clean laundry, fresh air, and warm wood. Safety and peace, with a smidgen of sugar cookies.

As different as it was—a log home with American country decorations, this place felt more comfortable to her than the house where she'd grown up, with its curtained windows and sick-room smells.

In spite of her earlier fatigue, there was no way she'd be able to sleep here. She'd snoozed a little on the plane and really zonked out in the car—probably more passed out than actual sleep, because she'd been pretty buzzed on bourbon when she'd decided to come. But it was a good decision. Getting away from Papa and Pequeño Zarigüeya for a while was just what she needed. And if she managed to help the distillery without having to be there? All the better.

The door to the room next to this one opened and shut. Brandon had showed her how the bathroom connected the two bedrooms. Now she heard the lock on her side click, and water running. It was surprisingly intimate listening to Brandon perform his nighttime routine. He brushed his teeth before unlocking her door again and leaving the bathroom. He would be kissably fresh when he crawled into bed—his brother's bed, since he was giving her his, because, he said, he knew the sheets were clean.

There had been a moment as he'd bid her good night when they both paused. He looked down at her, just inches away. His blue eyes warm and friendly, his body tall and strong in front of her, his scent enveloping her. She'd wanted to lean into him. She might have even swayed slightly forward. Maybe not. His mouth had quirked up, and he said, "Sweet dreams."

Dios, he was fine. And she'd caught him checking her out when she'd been dozing in the car on the way home. And there had been that almost kiss in the tasting center, although that could have been the alcohol.

Well, they'd be together for a whole week. And though she was supposed to be studying every aspect of the distillery, looking for cracks in the financial veneer, she looked forward to being a tourist. With the hottest tour guide in the state.

Bedsprings creaked when he lay down on the other side of the wall. There was a low murmur of voices from the television coming through. What did he watch before falling asleep? Sports? Movies? The news? *Porn*?

She rolled over, hugging one of the pillows against her midsection. It didn't really work as a human substitute, but it was as close as she was likely to get.

Traveling always roused her senses, and this trip seemed to be arousing her…sensations. The pillow pressed against her breasts, and her nipples hardened in response. Oh, no. She wasn't going to get busy with herself here in someone else's bed. At least not without his permission. She giggled a little at the idea of going next door and asking if Brandon minded if she masturbated with his pillow.

He would probably panic and have her on the next flight home before she knew what happened.

She sighed, and her stomach growled. The only thing she'd eaten since…wow, since morning, was a couple of cookies on the plane.

After sliding out of bed, she cracked the door to the hallway. Brandon had pointed the way to the kitchen, but told her he didn't know if there was much in the pantry, since the family wasn't due back for a few more days, and his brother and the girl next door had taken off on some sort of trip.

Tiptoeing into the kitchen, she flicked on a light that showed a vast space with marble countertops, dark wood cabinets, and an enormous kitchen table.

Opening the giant silver refrigerator, she found a drawer full of apples. She grabbed one, rinsed it in the sink, and then dug around a little more. There was a jar of peanut butter. That would work, but the loaf of bread on the counter was a few mold spores past its best-used-by date.

Hmm.

There was a clean spoon in the dish drainer next to the sink so she grabbed it, unscrewed the jar, and dug in. Smearing the peanut butter on the apple, she took another bite of the fruit. Her stomach sighed with joy. Not quite as exciting as snuggling up with a handsome American distiller, but as good a substitute as she could think of at the moment.

While she chewed, she perused the life of the Morgan family as indicated by the contents of their kitchen. It was about as homey as a place could get. She tugged at the collar of her night shirt.

Magnets from all over the world held photos and various papers on the refrigerator. There was a picture of a guy—almost as good looking as Brandon, but bulkier and with razored short hair, wearing military fatigues. He must be the warehouse-burning brother. There was also a picture of Brandon, in a suit and tie, accepting some sort of award. He looked really good. Happy, comfortable, pleased.

"I won the county volunteer of the year award," Brandon said from a few inches behind Lesa's right ear.

"Oh!" She whirled and smacked him in the face with a peanut-butter-coated apple.

"Ow!" He laughed, jumping back. "Sorry, didn't mean to scare you."

"Oops." She put the apple and peanut butter on the counter and reached for a paper towel. "I was just helping myself to your kitchen. And snooping."

"It's okay, really," he told her. "*Mi casa es su casa.*"

"I didn't realize you speak Spanish," she said.

"Oh, honey, I know how to say all kinds of things," he said, accepting the paper towel and swabbing at his chin. "I know '*hasta la vista, baby*,' and '*Una cerveza, por favor*'." He scratched his chin, with its day's end of scruff. "Oh. And '*Y'all know where el baño is*?'"

"Wow, that's quite impressive," she laughed. She was quickly falling in love with his accent.

He was adorable in his flannel sleep pants and white T-shirt. His feet were bare, and his long toes looked vulnerable on the cold tile floor. He smiled and glanced at the apple on the counter. "I'm sorry. I should have fed you dinner when we got off of the plane."

"I didn't realize how hungry I was until I got into bed," she admitted. "Here, you missed a spot." She reached up and ran her thumb under his bottom lip, scooping up a glob of peanut butter. Without thinking about it, she held it up in front of him.

He took her wrist and sucked the digit into his mouth. His tongue was warm and wet, stroking the pad of her thumb. Lesa nearly came from the sudden shocking sensuality of the gesture.

She gasped, and he released her hand.

"Oh, shit. I'm sorry. That was…that was weird." He picked up the roll of paper towels, then dropped it and grabbed her arm, tugging her toward the kitchen sink.

He flipped on the water and shoved her hand toward it. "Here. There's some hand soap around here—"

Lesa pulled back from the faucet and stopped him with a hand on his arm.

He froze, and their eyes met. Time stood still for a heartbeat, and then Lesa, feeling daring and bold, rose on her tiptoes and laid her lips against his.

He remained frozen. Eyes wide in shock.

For an endless, horrifying moment Lesa remained there, suspended in space, her lips glued to his unmoving mouth.

With a jolt she jerked away.

"So, um, okay. I guess I'll go back to bed now." She grabbed the remains of her apple and tossed it into the nearby trash can. "I'll, uh, see you in the morning. Sleep well!" she squeaked as she scurried from the kitchen and Brandon's motionless figure.

Chapter Five

Brandon awoke before sunrise as hard and aching as he'd been when he'd gone to bed just a few hours ago.

Damn. The memory of that kiss still had him wound up as tight as a spool of baling twine.

Lesa Ruiz had kissed him in the kitchen last night. Sort of. Okay, she *had* kissed him. But he'd turned into Chicken Boy. After sucking her finger into his mouth, he'd been mortified at his behavior, expecting her to slap him down for being inappropriate, so when she laid one on him instead, he froze. Only to lie awake all horny as fuck until nearly sunrise.

Peanut butter, apple, the surprise, the feel of her breasts brushing his chest—

And then she'd disappeared down the hall.

"Good night!" she'd called, before disappearing from his stunned sight.

He'd thought about following her, but the distinct sound of the door shutting behind her was enough to discourage him.

Bad idea. Bad, bad idea. She was probably still a little buzzed from the drinking they'd done earlier in the day.

And fatigued. She was his guest, and he'd pulled her slender finger between his lips and run his tongue over the ridges and grooves, sucking gently and then more firmly before realizing what he was doing.

Jesus. Just remembering the feel of her skin against his tongue had him twitching and dying for a repeat. A repeat and a further exploration.

Maybe she was just trying to ease the awkwardness with that little kiss. But who eased awkwardness with kissing?

He didn't need to do this, to get distracted from his goals by a woman. But she was so fun, sexy, and *appealing*.

It didn't matter. He had no business trying to puzzle out the intentions of a woman he barely knew before he'd had a significant amount of coffee. He wasn't going to sleep with her, no matter how much he wanted to.

Rising, he dropped his flannel pajama pants and pulled on clean khakis—damn. These were a little tight. He reminded himself to add an extra couple of miles to his next run. But hopefully the snug fabric would keep his still-enthusiastic morning erection from reaching out for her when he passed his bedroom, where she no doubt still slept. Damned thing was like a divining rod where she was concerned.

He found his running shoes and slid his feet into them without bothering to untie the laces, and shoved his wallet into his pocket. He grabbed one of Justin's sweatshirts from the back of a chair. Crockett Rockets? Justin must be getting nostalgic, if he was wearing their old high school's spirit wear. Most everything else he owned seemed to be Government Issue USMC. Shrugging, he shoved his arms into it and pulled it over his head, moving toward the kitchen.

He scribbled a quick message to Lesa.

After snatching his keys from the peg next to the door, he jogged to the car and started her up.

There was a heavy mist over the valley below him, but he

knew what was there—Blue Mountain Distilling, and a few dozen hard working friends and neighbors.

"Hey, Caleb." He greeted the distillery manager who slowed as he approached the main office building.

Caleb pulled off his Blue Mountain ball cap and ran a hand through his graying hair. "I saw you got home last night. Everything okay? I thought you were gone until Wednesday?"

"That's when the folks will be back. I came home early for business."

"Of course you did." Caleb frowned at him. "I'm surprised you lasted as long as a week on that boat."

Brandon grinned. "Well. It did have internet access, and I took my laptop."

The older man shook his head. "You need to get a life, son."

He had a life. Especially right now. "I actually brought a guest home with me. Lesa Ruiz, whose family owns Pequeño Zarigüeya tequila. We have a chance to make a deal with them, and I'm going to spend a few days impressing her with our rock-steady organization."

Caleb's expression didn't change when he asked, "Is that so?"

Uh oh. "What?"

He put his hands in his back pockets and rocked back on the heels of his ancient steel-toed boots. "Well now, you know about the rickhouse fire."

"Yeah. So do the Ruiz's. That's why we have to show her how great everything else is."

"The number three still sprang a leak, so she's down."

Great. Number three was the big still, the one that was used to produce their major product.

"How long is it going to be out of commission?"

Caleb looked toward the horizon, apparently calculating the difference between the last stars and the rising sun. "A few days. Depends on how long it takes to fix the hole in the roof that the welders are going to need to—"

Brandon cut him off. "Okay. We'll start in the bottling house."

"Uh, sure." Caleb looked doubtful, but Brandon didn't have time to find out what that was about.

He drew back into the car window. "I've got to go get my girls before the sitter charges me an extra week's fees."

"You'd better hurry. The fact that you got anyone to keep those two nut jobs is a miracle in itself. You should have to pay extra just for the pain and suffering," Caleb told him, stepping back from the car and slapping the roof. "I'll do what I can with the still."

Brandon drove on. Before he turned onto the main road, he looked back up the hill at his family's home. There was a spot a little farther to the north where he planned to build his own home someday. He'd always imagined a traditional farmhouse type deal—old fashioned with a big porch. But then that crap with Jamie McGrath and Suzanne happened. The humiliation still burned in his gut—the woman he was thinking of proposing to, asking her to move into that imaginary house on the hill, and her betrayal—he couldn't bring himself to start on the house, and it made sense to keep living with the 'rents a while longer.

He should revisit that house-building thing. Maybe it was time. He'd meet a nice girl one of these days—one who didn't have anything to do with the industry, and therefore would never have a chance to wreck his career, or his family's business.

He wondered what Lesa's long-term goals were. She'd told him that she'd like to travel. But didn't she plan to settle down some day? Take over her father's business? He felt a pang at the mental image of some handsome, dark-haired stranger with his arm around her as they laughed at the antics of their children.

Geez. He was losing it. Jealous of some imaginary man with the woman that he *wasn't* getting involved with.

· · ·

I went to pick up my girls, be back soon.

GIRLS? He had GIRLS? As in…children? Kids. Offspring. Babies. The sinking feeling in her chest was mostly likely her normal anxiety about being trapped by home and family. Which was crazy, because she was on vacation and not in the process of digging her roots in, but Brandon hadn't mentioned that he was a father in any of the conversations they'd had so far, and that was weird.

She looked around the kitchen and back toward the enormous living area. No signs of kid things. No pictures on the refrigerator, no toys underfoot, no stack of picture books on the bookcase next to the fireplace.

Well, she supposed, if he was an absentee father who didn't even tell people that he had children, it might follow that he didn't care enough to stock things to keep them entertained when they came to visit. But surely his parents—the kids' grandparents—would have pictures around.

There was a distinct hollowed-out dark spot in the middle of her chest, and Lesa tried to remind herself that her interest in Brandon was strictly casual. No matter how sexy the man was, she wasn't going to *marry* him, for crying out loud. There was the business associate part of things, but that was for her father and the tequileria. Brandon's relationship with his children—or lack thereof—shouldn't affect his business acumen, no matter how much she might want to *do* him.

She was supposed to be charming him into telling her all his secrets—his corporate ones, not his intimate ones. She had the sense that he was a straight arrow, but surely not everything here was as picture perfect as it seemed. Everyone, and every place, had weaknesses. And it was business, right? She knew she was going to have to suffer through a distillery tour and spend some time in the offices checking out the books, but she was hoping to get some vacation in before she bid him farewell and disappeared into the sunset. Kids would put a definite wrinkle in her ideas about what fun vacation activities involved.

Babies. She shuddered. They were awesome when they belonged to someone else, but they were just one more weight holding a person in place, and Lesa was born to be on the move.

She sighed and went back into the bedroom, and sank onto the bed.

She'd shown up in the middle of Brandon's scheduled time with his daughters, and they would probably hate her.

Maybe they'd like a present. If she'd known about them in advance, she'd have brought something wonderful, colorful, and Mexican from home. But what did she have with her that little girls would like? Surely they couldn't be much older than ten or twelve at the most—probably even younger—because Brandon was only about thirty, she guessed.

Her suitcase lay open on the foot of the bed.

Jewelry would be good, she supposed, but the only thing she'd brought was her mother's locket and a pair of gold hoop earrings. One earring per girl wouldn't cut it, even if they had pierced ears.

She had a couple of ceramic dishes that she'd brought as gifts for Brandon's mother and grandmother, but that was dumb. Kids would be bored and break them.

Her brand-new gold, high-heeled sandals peeped out from beneath her turquoise skirt. She pulled one of them out and admired its shiny leather straps. She'd splurged a whole week's worth of travel money on them, but they were so incredible, she hadn't been able to resist.

The shoes, and the adorable clutch purse that went with them. She didn't know if she'd have an opportunity to wear anything so nice while she was here, but they took up so little room in her suitcase, she'd indulged herself.

Well, girls liked to dress up. The shoes and purse had been expensive, but when she thought of meeting Brandon's girls, girls who didn't even have their own toys at their dad's house…she took the dishes from their gift bags and replaced them with the shoes and purse.

And just in time, it seemed, because she heard a car pulling up the driveway when she got back to the kitchen.

She took a deep breath. It was ridiculous to be so nervous. They were just kids, and Lesa was good with kids. Sort of.

There was the sound of one car door opening and closing, and then another, and then Brandon yelling, "Knock it off. I told you to stop that! I'm going to lock you in the garage before you've even met Lesa."

Oh, for heaven's sake. She wasn't so attracted to the man, or desperate to get Papa to sign a contract with him, that she would stand here and listen to him verbally assault his kids, no matter what they'd done. Her spine stiffened.

Plastering on a welcoming smile, she grabbed the gift bags and flung the door to the porch open and strode outside.

"Dammnit, girls, NO!"

Whaaaa?

A tangle of furry brown legs and ears turned at the sound of the screen door shutting and started to whine. Before Brandon could yell again, two enormous, slobbering, grinning bloodhounds broke free of his grasp. Leashes trailing, they bound toward the stairs. Toward Lesa.

In the next second, she was flat on her ass. Her brand new jillion peso shoes were being gleefully devoured—paper bag and all—by one dog, and the other swiped its enormous wet tongue over her face.

Chapter Six

"Damn, Lesa, I'm sorry," Brandon panted, as he fought to drag Maude away from her. He loved his dogs, but not everyone else cared to be licked to death.

"I guess they like the gifts," she gasped.

"Gifts? For them?"

"Oh, sure," she nodded, looking for a dry spot on her T-shirt to wipe dog spit from her face. "It's traditional."

Maude was momentarily distracted from molesting Lesa by Mabel's excitement, and Brandon turned to see what they were tearing apart. The remains of a couple of those fancy gift paper bags flew across the deck, and Mabel turned around to reveal a— "A purse?"

While he was trying to decide if he should take it from the dog, her sibling thundered back over to Lesa.

A quick glance told him that, whatever she thought would happen to them, the accessories were toast, so he pulled off his T-shirt and went to her, helping her to her feet.

"Lesa, I'm so sorry. Maude's not usually so, uh, attracted to women."

She stared at him, gaze scanning his naked chest before returning to his face. "So, um, these are your girls?"

"Yeah. You've met Maude. And that's Mabel." He pointed at the other hairy brat.

She took the shirt from him and swiped at her cheeks, holding it to her face for a long second. Was she crying?

"Did she hurt you?"

She jerked the shirt down. "No! I'm fine." But she was flushed, clearly upset.

He put an arm around her shoulders and brushed a strand of hair behind her ear that had come loose from its clip. That was when he realized she was laughing, not crying. Her shoulders shook, and the giggle she released made Mabel look up and bark happily. The dogs settled at her feet, alternately chewing on her purse and shoes, and staring up at Lesa like she was the second coming of the Purina fairy.

Turning his gaze back to Lesa, he noticed a strand of Maude slobber that she'd missed on her shirt, quivering as she laughed.

"Here." He took the T-shirt back and tried to blot the slooby goop—right over the slope of her breast.

"Oh!" She gasped, clutching at his bare shoulder. Her dark eyes were wide and shocked, but not dismayed, just— surprised, he thought.

His instinct was to pull away and apologize, but he realized Lesa's nipple was beaded under the fabric of the shirt he held. The soft weight of her breast in his hand made his already snug pants tighten. Her grip on his shoulder loosened, fingers stroking over the muscle there, sending a shiver down his spine.

Holding his gaze, she slid her fingers down his arm, over his hand, and pressed him tighter against her. Her lips parted, and he fixed on her mouth, so inviting, her tongue slipping out to moisten her lip.

Somehow his other hand held not only the dogs' leashes, but also her hip.

He pulled her closer, lowered his head to hers in the bright morning sunlight, and Mabel *woofed*, tugging at her leash.

"Damn!" He released Lesa and stepped away from her. "I'm so sorry."

"Why are you sorry?" she asked, brow furrowed, slow to let go of the hand that had been feeling her up. But she loosened her grip on his fingers and straightened her top.

Crap. Her nipples were staring at him as reproachfully as her eyes.

"I…we can't do this." He waved his hand back and forth between them. "It would be inappropriate, right?"

"Why?" Then her eyes widened. "Do you have a girlfriend? Oh. *Dios*, I—"

"No, I don't have a girlfriend," he hastily assured her. "But I shouldn't be manhandling you—"

"It's not manhandling if I like it," she interrupted, lips curved.

He groaned. "I'm trying to make a business deal with you, not—not *feel* you."

"Oh." She waved that away. "You're doing business with my father, not me. I'm just here as his corporate spy." She grinned. "I won't be signing any contracts, he will."

"But it'll be based on your opinion. And I don't want to influence—" Brandon stopped, realizing how arrogant that might sound. What? He might impress her so much with his seduction skills that she'd lie to her father about anything that she found unacceptable at Blue Mountain? And he wasn't going to sleep with her and then watch her eyes cloud when he offered to buy her father's distillery out from under her. "We need to have a working relationship, not a flinging relationship."

"Flinging."

"Yeah. The two don't mix."

"They don't." She quirked up the side of her mouth and put a hand on that hip he'd just been handling.

He groaned. This woman was torturing him. But he didn't do this stuff. He'd learned not to let his imagination take off—and definitely not his body—with anyone in the industry. It led to bad decisions.

It was a shame he *liked* her so damned much.

"We can start looking at the distillery today, if you're ready," he told her.

She shrugged. "I guess we should, huh?"

Wait, wasn't that why she was here?

"I mean, I want to see Kentucky while I'm here, too, you know?"

He did know that. And even though he had a little disconnect when he thought of taking off in the work week to play, going to play tourist for a while—with Lesa—held a definite lure.

He looked at the dogs, who had each laid claim to a shoe and were somehow managing to fight over the purse at the same time. Bits of leather and fabric were already stuck to the deck.

"I'm sorry about your stuff. I can take you to Macy's later and buy you new shoes."

Lesa snorted. "Oh, those old things? I bought them and only wore them once. They hurt my feet so much. I knew I couldn't bring food for the dogs through customs, and what do dogs love more than shoes to chew on? And a girl has to have a purse that matches, doesn't she?"

Brandon wasn't sure if the hysterical edge in her voice was because she was totally, completely lying—he'd never once mentioned his dogs to her—or because she was uncomfortable about what had just almost happened between them.

It didn't matter. He was ever so slightly in love, at that very moment, with his guest. Especially when she squatted down to give Maude a hug and didn't back off when the beast emitted an especially aromatic belch.

"So," she said, looking up at him. "I need to change clothes and wash up, but I'm ready to see the distillery."

Brandon nodded. "I thought we'd go to the bottling plant and look at the used barrels first, since that's probably the most interesting part to you, given the plans we're making." And because that was possibly the only part of the plant that was functioning this morning.

• • •

"Watch out!" Brandon pulled Lesa's arm and guided her out of the way of a barrel of bourbon as it rolled along tracks and into the bottling plant of Blue Mountain Distilling.

A burly man with a long scraggly beard tipped his imaginary hat at Lesa and gave the barrel an extra push through a low door and then bent to follow it through.

Brandon led her into the building through a normal door, and Lesa's senses were immediately swamped with the aroma of whiskey. "Whoa!"

Brandon smiled, hands in the pockets of his ever-present khakis. "Isn't it amazing?" He breathed in, and his firm chest in the gray Blue Mountain polo shirt rose, filled with the scents of his home. His pride was clear as he began to rattle off statistics about the numbers of barrels emptied to fill the bottles every day, how long different recipes were aged, and the process of moving the liquid from the barrel to the bottle.

"You seem to know every detail of the business," she observed.

He shrugged like it was nothing, but then said, "I've made it my mission to understand where every cent goes, and why it goes there, and how we can get it to have babies."

She laughed, but was blown away by his dedication. "You're not going to lose any of those extra cents either, are you?"

A shadow crossed his expression, and she thought he had turned to granite for a moment, but then he smiled, and said, "Yeah, I'm not really big on losing money."

Lesa already doubted that she'd find the dirt Papa was looking for, and learning that Brandon was such a meticulous businessman firmed them up. Based on the way he'd greeted each of his employees by name, he was a good employer, as well. Papa would do well to take some lessons from Brandon about how to run Pequeño Zarigüeya, rather than try to find a hole to burrow a snake into.

He led her to the other side of the room where empty bottles were moving around the machine that filled them with amber liquid.

"We recently replaced the old conveyor system with this newer, faster version. We had to hire an extra few hands to help with the increased production—capping, labeling, that sort of thing, but our output has increased enough to cover the cost, and we're actually up—"

A loud crash interrupted his explanation, followed by a shrill squeal. The conveyor jerked to a halt.

"What the hell?" He moved toward the source of the noise and found a man—Lesa thought his name was Caleb—squatting down and looking under a mass of metal, belts, and gears, waving away the stench of burning plastic. "What happened?"

Brandon fell to his hands and knees and crawled under the hulking mass of smoking metal with Caleb.

She could hear them discussing one thing that should have been attached to another thing, but couldn't really pay attention, because Brandon's pants were stretched across his incredibly fine backside. And then, suddenly, they weren't. Right before her eyes, the tan fabric gave way, slowly coming apart from his waistband and over his right butt cheek, exposing pink and green plaid fabric.

Pink and green boxers. How incredibly cute. Lesa hadn't considered what kind of underwear Brandon might wear—her vacation-addled mind had been spending a significant amount of time wondering what he might look like without them on at all. But the boxers were…perfect.

They went with his no-nonsense, conservative approach to life and business, but had a slightly whimsical edge, evidenced by the colors. Like a respectable family businessman who happened to own two ridiculously large, messy, loud dogs.

The conversation going on at her feet ceased, and the men under the machine began to back out slowly. Brandon paused. He hesitantly reached back, and touched the seat of his pants—the now absent seat of his pants.

"Damn!" he said, twisting to sit on the offending lack of fabric. And then, "Crap!" when he banged his head on the bottom of the conveyor system. He looked up at Lesa, embarrassment staining his cheeks, but he met her eyes with the calm dignity and professionalism she'd come to expect.

"What's the problem?" she asked. She should have been paying more attention to what he and the man were discussing. This was the kind of thing she was here to notice. What kind of problems were to be found at Blue Mountain, and how the staff dealt with them. Papa would want to know.

He shrugged. "Broken belt to the drive system. Caleb can fix it. He can fix anything."

Well that was anticlimactic. No million dollar systems failure to write home about, thank goodness. She really wanted this deal to work. "Okay, then. What should we go see now?"

He looked at his foreman, who shrugged.

"Maybe we should try lunch now. After I go put on some new pants."

"You don't have to change for me," she said.

Just a twitch at the corner of his mouth, but his eyes heated more than a fraction.

Caleb cleared his throat. "I'll just, uh, go find my toolbox," he said.

Chapter Seven

The city of Tucker was college-town America at its finest, and Brandon hoped Lesa thought it was as cool as he did. A series of small businesses lined either side of a wide, brick main street, and banners hung from the light poles, announcing the spring activities at the university.

Students wandered the sidewalks next to local residents, going in and out of the restaurants, boutiques, and bars.

He found a parking spot on the street half a block away from his destination: The Jukebox Malt Shop.

His grandpa had brought him here every other Saturday for years, buying him a chocolate malt and a cheeseburger that he still craved. Of course, half of the fabulousness then had been because he was getting to spend guy time with Gramps. Now it was because he wanted to show Lesa a slice of his personal history. Because it would sway her toward understanding how great the whole Blue Mountain experience was, not because it was about *him*.

He called bullshit on himself. If he was perfectly honest, he just wanted her to like him and like the things he liked.

Since the things he liked best were all associated with Blue Mountain, lunch in Tucker totally counted, he rationalized. And, he mentally continued, it would keep her from wanting to see all the parts of Blue Mountain that were, at that very minute, on the fritz. Like the still. And the roof. And now, the bottling machine.

"I think you'll like this place. Have you seen that show about the little dive restaurants? This is the one they should use as the gold standard. They always play oldies music, and they have the best cheeseburgers in the world," Brandon said, pulling the front door open so Lesa could walk in in front of him.

They were assaulted with full-blast, completely angry death metal—something about Jesus doing inappropriate things with the Buddha while Mohamed looked on.

Lesa turned to him with a raised eyebrow. "This is traditional, huh?"

At least that's what he thought she said. He had to read her lips.

The music suddenly cut off, and a complaint rose from deep behind the cook's window. "What the fuck, man?"

"There's old people here, dude," said the pierced and tattooed kid behind the counter.

Brandon looked around for the old people.

Lesa laughed. "*Amigo*, if you think twenty-five is old, then you are going to be in a nursing home much sooner than you want to be."

The kid may have blushed under the black eyeliner that had run and now streaked across his cheeks, but Brandon couldn't be sure.

"Sorry, dude. I just started here." He waved a bony arm around. "Sit anywhere you want. I'm Adam, and I'll be taking care of you. What do you want to drink?"

"I'll have a cherry cola, please. Lesa?" Brandon ushered

her to a table, and she slid into the seat.

"I guess I'll have the same," she said.

The kid—Adam—stood there, holding paper menus. "Uh, we don't have soda here."

"What? Why not?"

"Because that shit, er, that stuff is really bad for you. Sir." He pulled out his phone and tapped at it. "Here, look." He thrust the phone toward them. "There's like nine million pounds of sugar in one glass of pop."

Brandon looked at the graphic, with a baggie full of white powder on the table next to a can. He looked at Lesa, and shrugged. "Iced tea?"

"Chamomile or Lemon Zinger?"

"Do you have anything with caffeine?"

"Dude." The kid shook his head.

"Water will be fine." Lesa smiled and took the menus from the kid, handing one to Brandon. "How long has it been since you were last here?" she asked.

"A little too long, apparently," he answered.

"Because I think we're going to have a hard time getting a cheeseburger here."

The top of the menu had a red-highlighted note that read, "All of the food here is vegan, lactose-free, gluten-free, nut-free, and sugar-free, and prepared from locally sourced, organic, free-trade ingredients."

"I'm sorry. I really wanted to bring you to a good old-fashioned local restaurant, complete with heart attack and cancer-causing food. Do you want to go somewhere else?"

She shook her head, corner of her mouth tilted up. "No, that's okay. This is interesting, don't you agree?"

The woman did have some adventure in her. More than he did, but what the hell. He was still technically on vacation, where he'd promised his grandfather that he'd try to loosen up a little. He was more of a macaroni and cheese kind of guy than a wheatgrass drinker, but he was game, because she was game.

Adam brought two glasses of water—no ice—and put them on the table. "What'll it be?"

"I guess I'll have the farmer's delight salad," Lesa told him.

"Me, too." That sounded safe.

Adam nodded. "Okay. We're out of the vinaigrette dressing, though, because Shep—he's the cook—saw something on *60 Minutes* about how the mob is running the olive oil industry, and he's boycotting it."

"Can't you just use soybean oil or something instead?" Brandon figured Ranch dressing was out of the question.

"Dude. You don't want to eat too many soy products. All those plant estrogens will turn you into a girl." He looked at Lesa. "Not that there's anything wrong with that."

She tilted her head in acceptance of his apology.

"So what else do you recommend?"

Adam took the menu from Brandon's hand and looked it over. "I'm not really sure. Let me go ask Shep what we have. He's taking a cigarette break. He's totally hung over today, so he might not have gotten everything from the market."

Oh for chrissakes.

As Adam shoved through the swinging doors to the kitchen, Brandon pulled out his wallet. Throwing a five on the table, he said, "How do you feel about McDonalds?"

• • •

Instead of Arches del Oro, Brandon took Lesa to a falafel stand. Middle Eastern food had yet to come to her part of Mexico, so this was exotic for her. They sat in the town square, on a bench under a water tower of dubious structural integrity.

"Are you sure that thing's sturdy?" she asked, looking up

at the rusted underbelly of the tank.

Brandon shrugged. "It's been there forever. It's probably not gonna fall today. Besides"—he looked at the legs of the thing—"if it falls, we've got a 90% chance that it'll miss us and land over yonder." He pointed at another bench where a young couple sat, side by side, engrossed in their respective phones.

"Well that makes me feel better," she muttered, taking a big bite of fried chick pea balls and pita bread. Amazing. Swallowing, she asked, "Did you really use the word 'yonder' in a sentence?"

He grinned, causing her tummy to heat. Okay, it wasn't really her tummy, but she was in public and couldn't squirm. This man was really something. He was…genuine.

Lesa had quickly realized that Kentucky—this part, anyway—was a lot fancier than she expected from watching the television show *Justified*. Here there were stone or white board fences, open grassy fields scattered with horses, and nice cars driving alongside pickup trucks down the highway. But Brandon was still as down home as she might have predicted.

"My grandpa used to bring me to Tucker every other Saturday when I was little. We'd have lunch at the Jukebox, and then get ice cream from a guy who had a cart. I thought this was the coolest town in the world. I wanted to go to college here when I graduated from high school, because there were always guys playing Frisbee in this park, and I wanted to hang out with them." He indicated a couple of men tossing a disc back and forth, while a lab mix dog lay panting on the grass between them.

One of them wore a tie-dyed T-shirt and had a long gray ponytail.

"I think that might be one of the original guys I thought was so cool."

She swallowed and asked, "Is this where you went to

college?"

He shook his head. "Nah. I got a full scholarship to Louisville, so I went there instead."

"Do you regret not going here?" Lesa asked.

He looked around. "A little. It seems like a lot of people graduate and then stick around because it's such a nice little town. But then, I can't imagine staying here forever and not having moved back to Crockett County after graduation. Living in a whole new county—that might have been a little too much excitement for this homebody."

"Wow." Lesa didn't know what else to say. He was such a contradiction. So in-command, and sure of his place in life, taking charge of the situations that came his way—she'd seen that this morning when he'd dived right in to help work on the issue at the plant. Most other people would have been flustered and angry, but he just explained his solution and made other suggestions. Definitely large and in charge. But also willing to admit that he didn't like to be adventurous.

"What about you? Did you go to college?"

"Not really. I started—two semesters. But my mother was sick…for as long as I can remember, really. She had leukemia. It was kind of…like she was always a little bit sick, but then she got better, so I started college. Unfortunately, that was just the calm before the storm. It came back, and it came back pissed off. So I quit school to take care of her."

"But what about—and I'm not judging, just asking—what about your father, and your Tia Rita? Couldn't they help?"

She shook her head. "Papa worked all the time. He thought if he earned enough money he could find a cure, I think. And Tia Rita didn't move to live with us until after her husband died a couple of years ago."

"Oh, geez, sorry."

Yeah. So was she. She'd barely gotten a taste of life beyond Pequeño Zarigüeya, and she was still starving for more. She felt guilty, sometimes, for mourning her lost chances almost as much as the loss of her mother, but moving home had felt like crawling back into an airless cave. No light, no freedom. And no high-class diploma. "I managed to get a degree online."

He shrugged. "Nothin' wrong with that, if you learned what you wanted. Me, I learned how to come home and be a distiller's son."

What she had wanted was to learn how to escape the tequileria. She hadn't figured it out. "I think I'm about as different from you as it's possible to be."

"How so?" He crumpled the paper that had wrapped his sandwich and stuffed it into the paper bag that sat between them.

She suddenly felt guilty for not wanting to be like him. Someone who loved their home so much that they could never imagine leaving. "I want to travel. To see the world. When I was little, Mama and I would get books from the library and look at maps and talk about all the places we wanted to see. We were going to go to Italy, to Greece, Switzerland, then hop on a plane to China. All the places that weren't Mexico."

"That sounds cool."

"Yeah." She thought of her mother after she got sick, still looking at maps with her, even while she could barely sit up because of the chemotherapy. "She never got to go, but I told her I'd go for her." After she made sure that Papa and Pequeño Zarigüeya were secure.

He nodded, thoughtfully. "That cruise was the first time I've ever gone to another country. We've always taken vacations to all of the big American tourist places—Disney World, the Grand Canyon, the Statue of Liberty, stuff like that, but I've always had just as much fun at Lake Cumberland with a houseboat full of friends for the weekend."

He was so...centered. Peaceful. It made her nervous. "Don't you worry that you'd drown? That the houseboat would spring a leak and you'd wake up at the bottom of the water?"

He grinned. "I'm a pretty good swimmer. And I maybe slept with a life jacket on until I was fifteen."

She laughed with him. His blue eyes sparkled in the afternoon light and met hers. The heat she saw wasn't just a reflection of the noon sun. He was attracted to her, this simple, complicated man.

Holding her gaze, he reached out and twirled a strand of her hair around his finger.

She shifted and must have leaned forward, because his hand slid past her jaw, into her hair. Just for an instant, and then it was gone, but a trail of heat and energy remained behind. Her nipples beaded inside of her bra, and she fought the urge to cross her arms over her chest, lest she draw attention to her condition.

The breath left her chest in a huff, and she looked away, embarrassed at how much that simple touch affected her.

Clearing his throat, Brandon said, "So, uh, do you want to get some ice cream and then head on to our next stop? Or do you want to wait for the bourbon balls?"

"The what?"

"Haven't you ever had bourbon balls?" He stood and waited while she gathered her purse. Taking her lunch trash, he shoved it in the bag with his and tossed it to a waiting trash can, making a perfect basket.

"No, what's a bourbon ball?"

"Oh. Darlin.' You haven't lived. A bourbon ball is enough to make you give up your travel plans and move to Kentucky. It's a chocolate truffle with bourbon in it, and it'll rock your world. My friend Allie makes something called Brown Dog Balls, which are made with coffee and raw whiskey, and those puppies'll put hair on your chest. See?"

He turned and pulled the placket of his polo shirt apart,

and sure enough, she glimpsed a respectable dusting of golden hair.

She snorted. "I may have to pass on the Brown Dog Balls, then," she told him. But he should definitely keep eating them.

He nodded. "Good idea. But the bourbon balls at the place we're going? Eating those are as close to heavenly as eating—" Cutting himself off, he closed his mouth, and a bright red slash rose to each cheekbone.

"That good, huh?" Yeah, she knew exactly what he was going to say. And she had a definite urge to compare the two heavenly activities.

Chapter Eight

Lesa had, indeed, loved the bourbon balls. Vocally and sensually loved them. Had moaned and sighed and done everything except cry "more, baby, more," at them.

He promised to get his grandmother's recipe for her, and she left the candy shop with a chocolate smudge on her lower lip and a smile on her face. "Where to next?" she asked.

Anywhere you want, he thought, not for the first time. His cerebral cortex piped up and reminded him that he was supposed to be showing her the Blue Mountain books, or taking her to visit retail outlets in the area to show her how well-placed their products were.

But the parts of him that begged him to slide his hands around her waist, pull her against him, and kiss her senseless said, "What would you like to see?"

"Horses. Up close. We've driven by a million farms. I want to pet some."

He didn't even hesitate. "I know just the place."

• • •

She was delighted with the Kentucky Horse Park. She practically ran from stall to stall visiting each animal, cooing over the draft horses and thoroughbreds alike.

What had been a great spur-of-the-moment idea may not have been his best one, Brandon mused an hour later. The horse park had everything he remembered from coming here as a kid. Statues of famous racehorses, history, farriers and leather workers, and of course, horses. Which he'd half-hoped he'd outgrown being allergic to. As his eyes began to water and his nasal passages swelled, he felt like an ass. But he supposed he was in the right place. They kept horses *and* asses here.

"Ibe sorry," he told Lesa, after he sneezed for the hundredth time. "I'll go wait id the car, you go odd and see the foals."

"Nonsense," she told him. "Where's the gift shop?"

"I really dought thick I cad go shoppig right dow, but you go ahead."

He thought she shook her head, but his vision had gotten so blurry, he wasn't sure.

"Just sit here for a minute," she said, and shoved him at a bench.

"Honey, stay away from that man," he heard a mother tell her child. "He's spewing virus all over the place."

He wanted to protest and explain it was just an allergy, but he was too busy sneezing.

"Here." Lesa was back before he knew it. "I got you some antihistamine and some tissues." She handed him the little bottle. "Hang on, there's water here, too."

He managed to get the medicine opened and tipped the pills into his hand.

"Thagks," he muttered, swallowing the pills with a big chug of cool, kind, throat-clearing water.

Then he blew his nose.

"You okay to walk now?"

Brandon was glad Lesa remembered where they'd parked his car, because he could barely see his own feet. This was not a good feeling, needing to be led around by his arm. He should have known better. It had been years since he'd been around a horse—good thing they were bourbon people and not Derby folk, so he could avoid the beasts. Most of his friends and family went to Keeneland for the yearling sale, or Churchill Downs for the Derby each year, but he avoided both venues. He wasn't much of a betting man, anyway, so he hadn't realized the horses could still get to him.

Watching Lesa pet and coo over the animals was worth every tissue he needed now. She made as much of a fuss over an old grizzled draft horse with one eye as she did over the elegant Arabian. And his pain-in-the-ass dogs, for that matter.

They reached the car and Brandon dug out the keys.

"Oh no you don't," Lesa said. "You're in no condition to drive."

True. He could still barely see. He sneezed again and blew his nose.

"Let's get in and turn on the air conditioning. That'll probably help."

It wasn't particularly warm out, but running the air should filter out some of the horse dander in the local air. It was worth a shot.

He hated feeling out of control like this. His attempt to show Lesa what a fabulous business he was part of had already hit a few snags, and now he was reduced to a sniffling, teary, itching mess of hives.

Oh hell. He was breaking out in hives. He began to scratch.

"Brandon, your shirt is covered in horse hair. And so are your jeans. Hurry up, take them off." She tugged on his waistband, pulling his shirt up.

He started to laugh.

"What's so funny?" she asked, giving a hard yank that nearly took his head off.

"I've been fantasizing about you ripping off my clothes since I met you, but I was hoping it wouldn't be in a public parking lot," he said.

There was silence.

Brandon ran back over what had just come out of his mouth. "Well, the good news is, the Benadryl is taking effect," he said.

Lesa chuckled, maybe not as offended by his lame attempt at humor as he expected. A shiver ran over his skin that had nothing to do with allergic reactions.

She stepped closer, and he managed to focus well enough to see her smiling up at him, a come-hither look on her face if he'd ever seen one. And his dick was hithering. Oh, boy, was it hithering. Hither was the opposite of wither, right? Because he was getting hard.

Aw, geez. Her fingers slipped behind his belt buckle and began working the leather free from the metal clasp while she stared up at him.

He leaned to kiss her, but her mouth was so far away, he had to lean more, and then—

"Brandon!" Lesa caught him before he completely toppled over and pushed him back until he was more or less upright.

"How many of those pills did you take?" she demanded.

"I'm not really sure." Hey, so sue him. He was having an itching, sneezing, watery eyes and hives moment.

"Give me the bottle."

He dug into his pocket and pulled it out, handing it over.

She popped off the lid and looked inside. "There are three left. You started with twelve."

"Um, oopsie?" Brandon yawned.

"Yes, hello?" Lesa had her phone to her ear.

"Hi," Brandon said, finding his own phone and holding it up. "It's me, Brank." He was glad she was calling him. She was so pretty. He liked her a lot.

"Shhh." Lesa waved her hand at him. "I'm not talking to—yes, 911 operator, my name is Lesa Ruiz, I'm calling from the Kentucky Horse Park. I don't know if I need an ambulance, but my friend just took nine antihistamine pills, and he seems very confused."

"I'm not confused," Brandon argued. "I know exactly how I feel. I like you."

She smiled at him, a bright, sunshiney, happy girl smile, and he wanted to try to kiss her again. But she turned her back on him. That wasn't nice.

"Yes, I'll hold on." She turned to face him again. "I'm trying to find out if you're going to die of an overdose."

"An overdose! That's terrible! I don't do drugs. I never even tried to smoke pot when I was in—"

"Yes. Thank you. Yes. My friend was having an allergy attack, and he took nine antihistamine tablets." She looked at him. "He's about six feet tall and two-hundred pounds?"

"Six two and one-ninety," Brandon told her, hands on hips, indignant that she thought he was short and fat. He thought she liked him back, but maybe he was wrong.

She was still talking and listening to the person on the phone, but then she smiled again. "Thank you very much."

Pocketing her phone, she turned, pushed Brandon around, and marched him toward the passenger side. "The good news is, you're not going to die," she told him, opening the car door.

"Oh, thank God," he said, bending to get in.

"Wait." The command in her voice was clear, and it kind of turned him on. Maybe he should talk her into going back into the gift shop and buying a crop. She'd look really hot in black leather, with—

"You still have to take off your pants. You don't need

horse hair in your car. I'll put them in a plastic bag with your shirt."

She crossed her arms and tapped her foot while she waited for him to pull off his jeans. He got stuck when they fell to his feet and wouldn't go over his gym shoes, but she just shook her head and told him to sit down and take them off.

He finally managed to get his shoes and pants off and slid into the seat.

A second later, she was in the driver's seat. "Do you need help with your seat belt?"

"Nope." He managed to get it buckled. "You said I'm not going to die. If that was the good news, what's the bad news?"

"Besides me having to spend the next hour in a car with you wearing nothing but those ridiculously cute boxer shorts? You're going to pass out soon and sleep until…well, who knows?"

"Oh. Then I guess this isn't a good time to tell you that I decided we should fling, because my hither isn't withered."

And that was the last thing he remembered for many, many hours.

Chapter Nine

Late the next morning, Lesa sat in a rocking chair on the porch outside of the business offices of Blue Mountain Distilling and watched the sun fight for dominance in a wet, partially cloudy sky. Brandon was inside talking to the manager, Caleb, but Lesa had elected to wait outside. She figured he needed a break after she'd tried to convince him that she was crippled from having to carry his doped-up self to bed the night before. In reality, he'd managed to stagger in on his own, but as she suspected, he hadn't actually been awake.

The morning was glorious as a few victorious beams shot down to the walkway and shone against the cobblestones. A robin landed in the nearby grass and immediately scored something useful, because it carried its prize away, struggling under the weight of the heavy bug.

If she were in Mexico right now, there would likely be a lizard in their courtyard, sunning itself, waiting for its own unsuspecting critter. And if she were in Paris, it might be a pigeon. Same cycle of life, everywhere around the world.

It was a couple of hours earlier at home, so Papa would

probably just be turning on the television in the living room, settling into his big chair with a cup of coffee. Tia Rita would come in and nag him about the coffee rings on the end table, and he would pretend to agree to use a coaster and then put the cup right back down on the wood as soon as she left the room.

She missed him, but didn't miss the distillery. Of course, she'd just replaced one with another. But this was temporary. She'd do what she was sent here for, and then she'd be on her way. *Keep your eyes on the final prize*, she reminded her conscience. She'd find a way to prove to Papa that he should take a chance, do something different for a change and trust someone—Blue Mountain and Brandon, specifically, and then she could be free and clear, off to travel the world, like she wanted to do.

All alone, no one to be responsible for, no one to tell her what to do or how to do it.

Why did that thought depress her suddenly? Before, she'd always thought going around the world, working and living in different places would be so exciting. Like that woman—Julia Roberts played her in the movie—who took off from her regular life to eat ice cream and do yoga?

Before she was able to fully contemplate the fact that the Julia Roberts character ended up with Javier Bardem, her reverie was interrupted by the creak of a screen door.

Brandon stood in front of her, completely gorgeous in jeans. Jeans! All sixteen pairs (that was just a guess) of khakis must be in the wash. He did have on his ever-present knit polo shirt with the Blue Mountain Logo across one well-formed pec. He scratched his head. "Well, it looks like the still room is in the process of being dismantled so it can be put back together, so we'll have to pick back up there tomorrow, hopefully."

"That's okay." She stood. "We can start somewhere else,

if you want. One of the rickhouses?" Or not. She was already impressed with Blue Mountain. Looking at equipment and warehouses wasn't really up her alley.

That hand went back to his head, rubbing. "Yeah, so… that's having a little work done today, too." He looked up at her from under his eyebrows.

She already knew that one of the rickhouses had burned recently, and while she wanted to see the functional one, it wouldn't be a long-involved part of the tour and could wait. "What's broken?"

"The pressure regulator on the big still is…" He launched into an explanation of mechanics Lesa assured herself she could have followed if she'd really been interested. "And then we have to get the safety inspector out here to sign off on the repairs before we fire it back up."

He was being awfully forthright for someone who was supposed to be convincing her that Blue Mountain was in good financial shape. And it said something about Lesa and the people her family did business with that she was surprised to meet someone who was so…honest about issues he was having.

So no distillery tours today.

What a shame—*not*. They'd have to do something fun again. "How long will that take?" She found herself looking forward to spending more time with Brandon. What had he said yesterday? He wanted to fling. There was something about hithering and withering that she hadn't understood, but she was more than interested in finding out exactly what that had meant.

"It'll take another day or so to get things fixed up." He looked so distressed that she wanted to reassure him everything would be fine. She'd never met anyone who took his job so seriously.

She shrugged. "Okay. So what else can we do? What else

is there to this Bluegrass state besides horses, bourbon balls, and hot guys?" There were plenty more fun things to see and do around here. He was Mr. Travel Brochure, after all.

His eyebrows rose at that last part, but he didn't comment. Instead, he said, "Maybe we can drive to the Corvette museum this afternoon. A big ol' sinkhole sucked in a few cars there a couple of years ago, and I've been hankering to see what they did to fix that mess."

"*Hankering*? Really? And a sinkhole?"

There was that smile again. Oh. And a dimple.

Lesa didn't sigh out loud.

He tucked his hands in his pockets, which did interesting things to the way the fabric stretched across his lower body. "Yeah. I don't think Blue Mountain is in any danger, but there are all kinds of caves under the western part of the state, and I'd like to see what happens in a worst-case scenario."

Lesa shook her head. Leave it to Brandon to put the "work" into an afternoon of fun.

He smiled. "In the meantime, let's go over to the McGraths's and see if we can visit the site of the new business and tasting center. Eve and Lorena got in last night, and they can show us what we've got coming in the next few months."

Well, *that*, at least, sounded interesting.

The McGraths, Lesa remembered, were the other family that owned Blue Mountain Distilling. Lorena was the mother, the father and brother each having died a few years ago. There were two daughters, Eve and Allie.

"Do you want to walk or take the golf cart?" he asked.

"Oh, the golf cart. I love fast cars."

"Great. You'll love the Corvette museum, then." He reached his hand out to pull her to her feet.

His fingers were warm and firm around hers, and his scent wafted over her as she skipped a bit to keep up. His arm bumped into her shoulder, and she admired his strength, height, and contagious enthusiasm. He tugged her along, down the steps and over the stone path.

She laughed when she saw the cart. It was yellow with black racing stripes.

"You did say that you like fast cars, right?"

"Yes, yes I did."

"Well, baby, hang on!"

• • •

"Hello!"

Brandon watched Lorena McGrath open her slender arms and embrace Lesa in a welcoming air-hug-non-kiss that would have anyone less familiar with the Blue Mountain family believing that the women were long-lost sorority sisters.

Lesa seemed a bit surprised, but welcomed the embrace Lorena offered after Brandon introduced her as a potential business partner from Mexico.

Eve, his childhood friend and Lorena's oldest daughter, shot Brandon a look. From long experience he interpreted it as, "Look out, she's in Alexis Carrington mode." Alexis Carrington was the villainess in an eighties prime time soap opera, and while Lorena McGrath didn't often spend time trying to wreck other people's marriages, she was a major maternal control freak, rarely listening to anyone but her own internal fears.

Brandon figured the reason everyone tiptoed around Lorena was because they all understood where she was coming from. Losing her husband in a drunk driving accident was bad enough—but the scandal that followed had wrecked them all. And then losing Dave in Iraq—well, no mother should have to experience that. So she was cranky.

"I knew your parents long ago, dear," Lorena said,

leading the way into her living room and sounding more like a Southern belle than a modern, fifty-five-year-old businesswoman. "I was sooooo sorry to hear about your mother. I hope your father is doing well." The insincerity rolled off of her in waves.

Brandon noticed that Lesa's lips just barely tightened. "Thank you. Papa's great," she lied. Brandon wasn't sure how he could tell. Maybe a quick glance away before she answered Lorena, or a stiffening in her shoulders, but there was more there than simple grief at the long-ago loss of her mother.

He cleared his throat. "So we stopped down to see how the new tasting center is going."

"Oh, it's going to be gorgeous," Lorena gushed, reaching for a leather-bound notebook on the coffee table and opening it.

While Lesa oohed and ahhed over the architect's rendering, Brandon murmured to Eve, "What's going on?"

Eve motioned him to the kitchen. "The contractor's not answering my calls. Caleb said he hasn't seen him around in a few days, and I've tried calling him all morning, but no answer. And Mom's flipping out, because I hired the guy—he's an amazing carpenter—but he's someone she knew from her old life. You know how that goes. She's convinced he's a useless drunk."

"Yeah," Brandon said. He did know. Lorena had grown up in less than affluent circumstances, and after marrying Jamie McGrath had made herself into a bluegrass blueblood. And she didn't have much nice to say about anyone who'd known her when she'd lived in the rundown shack in the next county.

Just then, Eve's cell phone rang and Brandon returned to the living room.

"Lorena, I'm sure you're wiped out from all the traveling you've done the past few days."

"Oh, Brandon, you know me better than that," she said. "I never sit still."

Okay, exhaustion wasn't going to work as a ploy to keep her up here while the rest of them went to check out the work site.

"Anyway," he said, "I'm sure you have a lot to catch up with here at the house. I was going to suggest Eve take Lesa and me down to have a look and see how things are going."

"Do you mind if I use your bathroom?" Lesa asked.

"Certainly, dear." Lorena pointed her down the hall.

Brandon watched her walk down the hall—he loved to watch her walk.

"Dammit!" Eve said, swinging her phone like she was going to throw it, but she shoved it into her pants pocket at the last minute and shot a sideways glance at her mother instead. She opened the notebook she always carried with her—her life management planner, she'd explained to him once—and scribbled something in it.

"What's the matter?" Lorena was on full alert.

Brandon could see Eve weigh the wisdom of lying, and her decision to just get it out there in the open.

"There are two cement trucks down at the building site, and no forms in place for the foundation."

Ice crystals practically billowed from Lorena's nose and ears, and Brandon was glad Lesa didn't have to witness the woman go from a warm, welcoming junior league hostess to the ice queen who could freeze any obstacle in her path, damn the people who were collaterally frostbitten.

"Sweetheart," she said to Eve, "I apologize for not being more direct and pulling rank when it came to suggesting you should choose the more reputable construction company over a 'locally sourced' business. I grew up with that SOB and I knew his irresponsibility would stay with him."

"It's okay to just say 'I told you so,'" Eve grumbled under

her breath. Louder, she said, "Mother, I'll take care of it."

"I hope it's not too late to get the Randall brothers to come out and oversee the work. They did a wonderful job on the Robertsons' new house."

Eve sighed, and looked down the hall, apparently to make sure that Lesa wasn't standing there. She hissed, "Mom, the Randalls won't work with us. Apparently Daddy screwed them over, too." She turned to Brandon. "Sorry. I know you don't like to have to talk about that stuff."

Brandon shook his head. "No problem." And it shouldn't be. It had been many years, and the pain of humiliations past was beginning to finally ease. Except, of course, when anyone brought it up.

Lorena's lips were tightly closed. There was no way she'd call the Randall brothers now. Lorena had lost not only her husband in that drunk driving accident, she'd lost a shit ton of money and, even more important to her, significant social standing—and was only now beginning to feel comfortable in all of the places that fashionable Kentucky women went.

"Well. We're not going to be bringing that dirty laundry out for airing." She turned. "Oh, look, here's your friend."

Lesa raised an eyebrow. "Uh, yes. Here I am."

Eve rolled her eyes, and Lorena's lips were even whiter than usual.

"We'll go down and talk to the cement guys and see what we can do," Brandon offered. Another instance where Lesa would see Blue Mountain at her worst, but there was nothing he could do about it now. At least she didn't have to be present for Eve and Lorena's fight about who the contractor should be.

Eve said she'd keep trying to reach the contractor, while Brandon and Lesa took the golf cart down the hill. As far as he knew, Lorena stayed in her perfect living room with a frozen smile, trying not to let her facade crack.

• • •

Over the next several hours, Lesa learned more about the construction business than she had ever hoped to. Right now, she was watching concrete dry. Or set. Or cure. Whatever. And surprisingly enough, she was enjoying herself immensely.

"You're gonna have to pay for these two trucks and the two more that are on the way," the cement mixer driver had told Brandon when they rolled the golf cart up to the building site, which was nothing more than a hole in the ground at the moment.

"You can't divert it to another job?"

"Nope." The man sent a stream of brown spit into the foundation hole for the new business and tasting center for Blue Mountain Distilling.

"Why not?" Lesa asked. Not to challenge the man—she was trying to remember that this wasn't her problem, though she did feel bad for Brandon having to deal with this. He hadn't said so directly, but she got the impression Eve was in over her head on this project, and he felt responsible to help her dig out. His enthusiasm for the project was infectious, however.

The cement driver smiled at Lesa, looking her up and down. Brandon stepped closer to her.

She'd never admit it to anyone but herself, but his protectiveness gave her some warm fuzzies. And there was that time when they first met—when she misunderstood what he told her his job was and she thought he was a professional grocery shopper. The dentist had laughed at her, but Brandon had shot him daggers with his eyes and gone along with her confusion so as not to embarrass her. The warm fuzzies squirmed happily. She smacked them down and took what she hoped was a casual step away from Brandon. Snuggly safe feelings could be deceptive, leading to dependence—and obligation. She was on vacation here, not *The Bachelorette*.

"Well, ma'am," the guy said, "This here ready-mix is a moderate-weight aggregate, and the other job we have in this area today is for a decorative, stained mix, and we can't just dump extra rocks and pigment into this particular version. And concrete don't keep. Once it's been mixed, it's hardenin'." *Spit.*

"How long do we have before you have to dump it?" Brandon asked, eyeing the giant hole in the ground and the half-finished forms for the walls of the basement.

The guy looked at his phone. "'Bout an hour."

"All right." He motioned to the small finished area in front of him. "You start here. We'll put up the rest of the forms and hopefully keep ahead of you."

Spit. "Welp, son, I hope you've got some work gloves, or those purty hands o' yours are gonna be in sad shape by about three this afternoon."

Caleb, the distillery manager, had been listening to Brandon, and he nodded. "Miss Lesa," he said, "would you feel comfortable driving up to the bottling plant and then the still room, and ask everyone who's not fixing the broken equipment to get their backsides down here?"

"Absolutely," she answered. "Especially if I get to drive the race cart." Shooting Brandon a grin, she jumped into the driver's seat of the golf cart.

"Hang on," he said, walking over to her. "I'm sorry. I'm gonna be tied up with this all day. I can ask Lorena—" He shot a worried glance back toward the McGrath house. "Maybe Lorena and Eve would be free to take you into Lexington to go shopping or something?"

Lesa snorted. "Where will I find extra work gloves? We don't want your *purty* hands to get too beat up. Or mine."

"Ask Dale in the still house," Caleb hollered, as she drove away, leaving Brandon staring after her.

The next four hours were a whirlwind of hammering and mud. What normally probably took two days of work was finished before the last concrete truck rumbled into the driveway of Blue Mountain.

"Oh my God, you're a mess," Eve said, handing Lesa a wet wipe to clean her hands. She'd been on the phone for hours trying to straighten things out with the contractor. "I can't believe you got down in there and set those forms with the guys. I'm in awe."

Lesa shrugged. "I mostly was a…chipmunk," she said.

"Gopher?" Eve asked. "You go for this and go for that."

Lesa laughed. She liked Eve. "Yes. I goed for…um, went for tools. But I did manage to get dirty enough for it to count, I guess."

"I'll say."

Lesa dropped the wipe into the plastic grocery bag Eve held and thanked her for the bottle of water she handed her. The woman was about her height with short dark, wavy hair and blue eyes. She reminded Lesa of Elizabeth Taylor—somewhere between the teenager in *National Velvet* and the man-eater in *Cleopatra*. Maybe *Father of the Bride*.

She wondered if Brandon had ever had a thing for Eve, but when he walked over and asked her about the contractor, she didn't get any vibe from either of them about anything besides friendship. Not that it was any of her business. She was a temporary guest star in this film.

"So did you find him?" he asked.

"More or less. He's apparently had the flu. According to Mother, it's the brown bottle flu."

"Aw hell." Brandon started to scratch his head, but stopped and pulled off his glove before trying again.

Lesa noticed his hands didn't look the worse for wear. Too bad. She wouldn't have minded rubbing lotion into his blisters, if he'd gotten any. But she suspected, from the way he'd taken on the manual labor, that he was no stranger to hard work. He was just better at the business part of things, so that's what he did.

"Did you fire him?" he asked.

Eve shook her head. "We don't have anyone else who can step in right now, and we're already behind schedule, which really will put us over budget." She shot a look at Lesa.

Lesa pretended to be busy checking her phone for emails and not paying attention.

In spite of the broken equipment and mismanagement in the construction arena, she felt that this was a good place. The people here jumped right in to solving problems. When she'd stepped into the still room, people had been cleaning— not sitting around and drinking coffee while they waited for their actual job to start. And when she'd explained that Brandon needed help with construction, one of the women had laughed and said, "Yeah, I would imagine he does." And then she'd told Lesa a story about the pinewood derby car he'd tried to carve when he was a Cub Scout.

Brandon wasn't just the big boss's son. He was a respected, contributing part of this enterprise. His employees cared for him, and he cared for them as well. And that seemed like good business to her.

Granted, Lesa hadn't yet bothered to dig into the operations and finance books, but her instincts told her that Papa could do worse than go for Brandon's barrel deal. Without all the subterfuge.

She looked at Brandon, wiping sweat from his brow with the back of his hand, his polo shirt stretched over his sweaty chest and shoulders, and reminded her hormones that it was all fun and games on vacation, but thinking about more than a fling led to people getting hurt—like her. Brandon was exactly the kind of guy who would want his woman to stick close to home, and she'd already discarded that as a life option.

Chapter Ten

"Oh my God," Lesa gasped between licks and sucks at her fingers. "This barbecue sauce is amazing. I. Love. It."

Brandon shot a glance at the pile of bare rib bones on her paper plate. "I can see that."

The rest of the afternoon's work crew bid Brandon and Lesa good-bye and faded into the dusk with a wave.

What a great group of employees they had here at Blue Mountain. They'd pitched in to help him get the forms in for the foundation and even pretended to protest when he insisted on buying ribs and beer as a thank-you.

It had been a good day. It could have been a major setback for Eve's project—and this tasting center was near and dear to her heart—but they'd managed to pull together to take care of today's crisis, anyway.

Hopefully she'd be able to get her contractor sobered up long enough to come through and finish the job so she didn't have to listen to her mother gripe too much. And so they didn't have to have a public dissection of past problems, and why some in the tri-county area wouldn't do business with Blue

Mountain. The last thing Lorena wanted was to talk about her late husband. Brandon's memories of Jamie McGrath were tarnished, as well. He didn't like to remember how gullible he'd been when he'd gotten involved with Suzanne, and what she'd gone and done, the part she'd played in Jamie's downfall, but it wasn't about him. What he couldn't bear was the thought of Lorena and her daughters being dragged back through the crap of the past.

Lesa seemed to have had a good time helping this afternoon, too, which surprised him. He could tell she was a doer. But getting in that big muddy hole and slogging around all day certainly wasn't in her visiting-business-associate agenda. If she was playing him so that he'd offer Carlos below market price on the barrels, she was working overtime. And there wouldn't be any payout. He let himself have a moment to imagine Suzanne, standing and watching while Brandon and the rest of the Blue Mountain crew worked. No, Suzanne wouldn't have been standing and watching. If she'd stuck around at all, she'd have been sitting in a folding chair searching Pinterest for fingernail decorations.

"And this beer is pretty good, too." She swallowed the last of the Bourbon Barrel Ale in her bottle and clunked it down on the table. She grinned, a stray bit of sauce on her cheek, giving her a definite sexy maniac look. Kind of a supermodel Hannibal Lecter thing.

"You've got a—" He touched his face, to show her where the sauce was.

"Where?" She reached up, but only managed to smear it farther along her cheek.

With an exaggerated sigh, he swiped at her face with his thumb and held it out in front of her.

"Oh." She reached out, took his wrist, and pulled his thumb into her mouth. Watching him, her tongue swirled over the pad, silky strokes along the knuckle.

Oh Jesus. He shifted in his seat

With one last little lick, she released him. "There." "We seem to have a habit of cleaning each other's faces," he said, remembering the other night in the kitchen with the peanut butter.

She snickered. "We're like orangutans at the zoo." She held up the bottle, and raised her eyebrows at Brandon. "Want another one?"

He shook his head. He still had to maneuver the golf cart up the hill.

She frowned in thought. "Are orangutans the ones that have big swollen butts when they are in the mood?"

"Are you sure you want another?" he asked.

She nodded vigorously. "This is the best beer I've ever had."

"It is good. But I think we're out of cold ones."

"Oh. Maybe another would be a bad idea, anyway." A strand of hair fell over her face and she blew it out of the way. She smiled, and it was *that* smile. The one that welcomed everyone in. A little goofy at the moment, but still powerful.

He knew she wasn't for him, that she was a rambler, and she said she didn't want to live at a distillery. Although she might feel differently if her dad's enterprise was in better shape. He'd gotten some information today about the Ruiz finances that told him that Pequeño Zarigüeya could use more than some souped-up barrels. They needed a cash infusion. If he were inclined to take risks, he might be able to help, in exchange for an interest in the tequileria. He wasn't sure it would be a good deal, however, and he only took chances if—well, he didn't take chances.

He gathered the rest of the trash and shoved it into the big garbage bag and made a mental note to send the owner of Mamaw's Meat Shop a bottle of Dangerous Dave's as a thank-you for the last-minute delivery. Mamaw's was another of his favorite hole-in-the-wall places—fortunately this one hadn't been taken over by smoking, drinking, organic, Goth people.

"What are we going to work on tomorrow?" she asked.

"Uh, hopefully nothing," he said. "I'm supposed to be convincing you that everything here is hunky dory, not roping you into participating in our problems." The last thing he needed was letting her see anything else go wrong.

"Hmm." She eyed him, but didn't say anything as she rose to follow him to the golf cart.

It was early spring, and while the sun fought to leave streaks of color in the western sky, it still went to bed fairly early.

"Brr!" Lesa shivered, pulling the sleeves of her new Kentucky Horse Park sweatshirt over her hands and crossing her arms.

"Here." He started to pull off the zippered hoodie he'd dug out of his backseat, but she shook her head.

"This is better," she said and slid her arms around his waist, tucking her head against his shoulder.

Yes, yes it was, although a small part of his brain reminded him that he wasn't going to get involved. He hesitated, then pulled her close and led her down the sidewalk.

"Oh, look!" She pulled away from him and slid a box from her pocket. "I still have a bourbon ball from yesterday." She shoved the candy into her mouth.

He wished he could see her face clearly, but she was backlit, and he could only hear her groan. Followed by soft whimpers and moans.

He waited, trying not to notice that everything she did turned him on. If this was what she sounded like after a good meal, a few beers, and some chocolate, what would sex sound like? He wished for the ninetieth time that day that she wasn't there on business, that she was his, even just for the week.

"Omigodomigod," she murmured, finally. "That was amazing. As amazing as today and almost as wonderful as you."

She stepped back toward him and put those slender arms around his waist, looking up at him. They'd turned slightly, and he could see her better now. The invitation in her eyes was clear, and the way she pressed those curves against him was unmistakable.

"Lesa…" He should fight the need she brought out in him every time she was near.

"Brank," she giggled. "Yesterday, you said you wanted to fling with me. That your hither wasn't withered or something."

Shit. Had he actually said that? He thought that might have been a Benadryl-induced hallucination. "We've had a few beers, and I don't want to take advantage—"

She drew back and looked at him. "I like you. This is the best vacation I've been on in forever, and…I like you."

She looked at his mouth, then away, then back again, biting her lower lip.

"I like you, too."

Her eyes were clear and sharp when they met his, and he knew that she meant what she was saying. So did he. The thought that he'd been here before, believed a woman who said she really liked him, flitted through his mind, but then the scent of limes and oranges and sunshine washed over him in the evening breeze, and he had to get to the source. Had to. He was done. Waving the white flag of surrender to his better judgment, he put one arm around her waist and threaded the other hand in that long, silky hair. He cupped the back of her head, leaned down, and kissed her soft, inviting lips.

And she kissed him back, mouth slightly open, welcoming him. Sweet chocolate, bitter beer, and tangy barbecue sauce met his senses as he nipped at her lips and licked into her mouth. She let out a tiny whimper, so he hesitated—and she protested his retreat. One of her arms curled around his neck and pulled him down for more, fingers stroking his neck, the other arm around his waist, holding on to him, clutching at the fabric of his shirt.

The evening could have turned cold and windy or wet and hailing for all he was aware of anything but her. He shouldn't be touching her, there was some reason he was supposed to stay away from her—something to do with his life and responsibilities here at Blue Mountain, but he'd be damned if he knew what the problem was. Instead, he was pretty sure he could kiss her forever.

Her breasts pressed against his chest, and every beat of her heart was answered by a jolt from his own. Blood pumped to his skin, his lips, his groin, making him desperate for more. She moaned as she arched her pelvis against his thigh. Surely she could feel the effect she had on him. He longed to rip away the layers of fabric separating them.

He broke away, panting for breath.

Lesa stared at him. "It's a good thing you're sober," she told him. "Because I think we need you to get us back to your house."

He dug his keys from his pocket and beeped open the doors. "Let's hope you still feel that way when we get there."

• • •

"Well huh."

Lesa looked up to see what Brandon was *huh-ing* about. She'd been watching the last streaks of day fade behind the mountain, because every time she looked at him, she wanted to finish what they'd started on the other side of the hill.

There was an immense motor home filling the flat parking area next to the house and a little SUV next to it. It appeared every light in the house was turned on.

"My brother's home."

Well, there went all of Lesa's plans for the rest of the night. She wanted Brandon with every fiber of her being, and she knew he wanted her, too. Every look, every touch, every word they exchanged was loaded with attraction.

"I wonder if Allie is still helping him out," he mused.

"Eve's sister?"

"Yeah. Justin banged up his leg a couple of weeks ago, and she stayed with him to help take care of him and then somehow convinced him to travel halfway across the country on one of her goofy schemes."

His smile was fond, so clearly he thought her goofy schemes were okay. And Lesa felt a vague wash of jealousy spread over her.

"Are you okay?" Brandon put his car in park and looked over at her. "You have a funny look on your face."

"I'm fine." *Just…jealous.* Which was weird, because she absolutely didn't want this life, with all of this family responsibility to smother her. They just all seemed so…happy. Even crabby Mrs. McGrath had a certain serenity about her.

Lesa's parents had loved her. Papa still did, she knew. And she had Tia Rita and cousin Raoul. But there had been so much sadness after Mama died. It was like she took all the joy with her when she died. The Morgans and McGraths had experienced loss, too. Eve and Allie's brother and father had both died. But there was still friendship and joy and laughter, even in the midst of the drama of the past day. "Let's go see what's going on."

They were met at the top of the stairs by two anxiously whining dogs.

"What's the matter, girls? Did Uncle Justin put you out and not let you back in?" He squatted down and made kissy noises and rubbed ears and scratched back ends.

Mabel and Maude were in ecstasy, and now Lesa was

jealous of them, too.

A female scream rent the night air.

"What the hell?"

Brandon rose to his full height, flung the door open, and ran into the house.

Lesa was hot on his heels, but the dogs passed him before he made it to the arch from the kitchen to the living room. Where he stopped.

Lesa crashed into his back and they tumbled to the floor, landing in the middle of…a tangle of arms and legs and other body parts. Naked body parts. And very exuberant dogs.

"Get these fucking mutts out of here, you asshole," bellowed the man attached to that— *Whoa*. Lesa would have closed her eyes while she tried to extract herself from the pileup, but she didn't want to accidentally put her hand down on the wrong thing while she scrambled away. She did pause to allow herself to wonder if that sort of endowment was genetic and shared by brothers, however.

The female half of the naked people—Allie, Lesa assumed—was laughing and swatting at the dogs, who were swiping her face with their enormous tongues, fighting for the right to slobber on her more.

But they quickly realized that Lesa was there, too, and one of them—Mabel? Maude?—turned to share her generous affections.

Somehow, Brandon managed to grab a quilt from the back of a nearby chair and got it to Allie, who wrapped it around herself. Then he grabbed the dogs and began to pull them away. Justin sat with a pillow over his lap, glaring at Brandon, the dogs, and then her.

"Who are you?" he growled.

"Be nice," Allie chided, tossing Justin a pair of shorts.

Lesa decided not to take it personally. They had interrupted something pretty astounding, to have produced that kind of a scream from Allie, a very pretty strawberry blonde.

Now that Justin was decent-ish, Lesa took a closer look at him. He was as good looking as Brandon—the same blue eyes, the same high cheekbones, and light brown hair. But where Brandon was almost pretty, Justin was rougher looking. Brandon had told her his brother had served in the military, and it showed.

He was also very bulky and tattooed.

"I'm Lesa Ruiz," she told Justin, reaching to shake his hand.

"Do you mind?" Instead of taking her hand, Justin twirled his finger to indicate that he'd like her to turn around.

"Oh!" She swirled.

The woman snorted. "God. It's just a dick."

"It's a really nice dick," Justin protested.

"It's not like she hasn't already seen it. Hi, Lesa. I'm Allie McGrath. Ignore Sergeant Surly there." She reached a hand to help Lesa to her feet, holding on to her makeshift sari with the other.

Brandon had managed to shove the dogs through the door to the basement and slammed it shut, in spite of howling, whining protests.

"So," he said, coming back into the room, a grin across his face.

"Don't start," Justin said, apparently dressed now, from the sound of a zipper behind her.

Brandon took Lesa's hand and turned her so they were both facing his brother, who sat, arms crossed over his chest. One ankle was wrapped in an elastic bandage, the other leg was stretched in front of him.

Justin waved a hand, dismissing Brandon. "It's no big deal. Mom and Dad already know, so there's no need to get on social media and start spreading gossip."

Allie gasped in mock outrage. "It is *so* a big deal." Then she snorted. "At least it was a few minutes ago."

Lesa coughed a laugh.

Justin reluctantly let a smile curve his hard mouth to the side. "Yeah, well. I guess it's kind of a big deal to me, too. Just don't say 'I told you so.'"

Brandon turned to Lesa and explained, "I told him he and Allie were meant for each other."

Justin looked from Brandon to Lesa and to their clasped hands. "So. Anything *you* want to share?"

Chapter Eleven

Brandon hadn't realized he was holding Lesa's hand until he dropped it at Justin's question. "No. I mean, nothing like—" He cut his eyes to Lesa, who was patiently watching him, expressionless. Did she think they were—did *he* think they were…? They certainly had been *about* to be…if only his brother and Allie weren't here.

She smiled and turned back to Justin and Allie. "I'm Lesa Ruiz. Brandon allowed me to invite myself to your home to visit Blue Mountain Bourbon and determine the suitability for a business agreement with my father's company, Pequeño Zarigüeya—Little Opossum Tequila."

"Oh." Justin shot him a look, one that promised brotherly retribution for the coitus interruptus. But then he put on his big boy face and said, "I'm interested to hear your ideas."

"You are?" Brandon couldn't help himself. Justin had spent the last twenty-odd years of his life trying not to be involved in anything to do with the business.

His brother shrugged. "Well, you know. If I'm going to be around, I might as well know what's going on."

Huh. Hooking up with Allie must have changed his mind about moving out west. He'd have to thank her later.

Allie, who'd grabbed her clothes and run out of the room wrapped in the blanket, came back, fully dressed and folding the quilt. "It's nice to meet you," she said, dropping the quilt on the back of the couch and shaking Lesa's hand. "Blue Mountain is an awesome place, and I'm sure you'll find plenty to impress you."

Brandon hoped so. It hadn't gone so well to this point, not with half of the production equipment on the fritz.

He really needed to find a few more touristy things to do to keep Lesa's attention off of the malfunctions until they were straightened out.

"We met with Lorena and Eve this morning to see the plans for the new tasting center, but got side tracked by *building* the new tasting center, so..." He trailed off when Justin and Allie exchanged a glance.

"Was my mom okay?"

Was she ever? The woman was never relaxed, so it was hard to tell. Then it dawned on him. "Is this"—he wagged his finger back and forth between Justin and Allie—"is this not sitting well with Mrs. McG?"

Allie shrugged. "Nothing sits well with my mother. But Eve got her an appointment for a full spa day tomorrow."

That might help. Lorena McGrath was the hardest working woman in the universe—she'd made sure that her books were spotless after she took over when her husband died and left her with that mess—and she could put on the grace and charm when dealing with the media and business competitors, but she was a stone-cold bitch when it came to the Blue Mountain Bourbon family—including her own daughters. Eve was the only one of them who could, if not manage her, at least keep her in check. Usually.

"Have you toured the plant yet?" Justin asked Lesa.

Lesa shot Brandon a look, but before he could spew his line of excuses, she said, "We'll be checking it out in a few days. First, I've made Brandon promise to show me all over this wonderful state of yours."

"What are you going to see?" Allie asked.

"I was going to ask if we could go to a race, but the Horse Park didn't work out so well," Lesa said. "What would you suggest instead?"

"Wait. You went to the Horse Park?" Justin's eyebrows rose to his nearly nonexistent hairline. "You, Benadryl Brandon?"

"Uh, yeah."

"Did you not remember that you're allergic to horses?" He shook his head. "Dude."

Brandon cleared his throat. "I hoped I'd outgrown it." Geez. It had been bad enough waking up from his accidental overdose. Getting to relive the embarrassment was excruciating.

"Dude," Justin repeated again. Between that and the all-purpose f-bomb, his brother didn't need many more vocabulary words.

"I might have been a little too pushy about wanting to go," Lesa said. "Brandon was being polite, I think."

Well, that and too blinded by lust for you, he didn't say.

"Do you remember that time you tried to get your horsemanship badge in Boy Scouts?" Justin laughed. "We had school pictures the next day, and you were so swelled up that Grandma Morgan didn't know who you were when she got the pictures."

"Gee, bro. Thanks for that reminder. Maybe you can pull out the photo album."

"Oh! Great idea!" Justin stood and limped toward the bookcase.

"Halt!" Allie pulled a bag of chips from a box on the

kitchen table and carried it into the living room. "Not to change the subject from Justin's attempt to torture you, but what do you say we see what's on Netflix?"

• • •

Lesa had almost as much fun watching a *Gotham* marathon with Brandon and his brother and Allie as she would have had her other plans for the evening come to fruition—finishing what they'd started at the building site.

She never, ever sat at home and watched television. That was Papa's domain. The darkened living room, the blue light cast over everyone's features, normally gave her a case of the moodies. She liked to read at night. When she went out, it was to Puerto Vallarta with Raoul and other employees from the distillery. She didn't like to watch television; it made her sad. She told herself that she'd rather live life than watch it piped into the living room.

But here it felt comfortable.

As it was, she felt like a schoolgirl with a crush sitting next to Brandon on the couch, wishing he would put his arm around her. Especially after Justin and Allie had piled into a large recliner together under her dressing-gown quilt.

If they'd been alone, she might have laid her head on Brandon's shoulder and traced patterns on his thigh until he lost complete track of the TV show, but instead, she settled for leaning the other way and tucking her bare feet under his leg.

Her ploy worked. After a surprised glance her way when he felt her toes slide between him and the couch, he smiled and put a hand around her calf before turning back to the TV. Fortunately, she'd remembered to shave that morning.

But after an episode and a half of watching the future Penguin waddle around after Jada Pinkett Smith, Lesa was getting restless.

Brandon still had his hand on her leg, but other than the occasional stroke of his thumb along her shin, he completely ignored her. His touch sent shivers all the way to the base of her skull...with a few stops in between. She needed to squirm, but didn't want to dislodge his hand. That touch, that relatively small point of contact, had become the center for every erogenous zone in her body.

She didn't dare move the calf he held, but her other leg, the one closer to his hip, might just need to stretch. As nonchalantly as possible, she slid that foot from under his thigh and reached it right across his lap.

And wouldn't you know it? His right hand grabbed that foot and held on to it.

Now those shivers were traveling up both of her legs and meeting in the middle. She arched her back, because the tension was beginning to take on a slight throbbing ache.

And still he didn't look her way. But if she wasn't mistaken, there was a distinctly firm shape under that ankle on his lap. She shifted her leg a tiny bit and he stiffened—both his shoulders and his erection. *Bingo.*

She watched him stare at the television. He was fixed on a commercial for some sort of miracle cleaning product and so busy not noticing her that she was sure he registered every breath she took.

"Hey, guys, I think we're going to go to bed," Justin said. Allie rose from his lap and Justin followed more slowly, his injured leg still apparently causing him discomfort.

Lesa started to pull her foot back from Brandon's lap, but he held it in place, still not looking at her.

Her breath sounded shaky when she wished the others a good night, but they were so wrapped up in each other, giggling and touching, they didn't seem to notice.

"We'll just crash in the camper, since all of our stuff's still out there," Justin said.

"Good, because I'm using your room since Lesa's in mine," Brandon told them.

Justin looked at her. "Make sure you lock that connecting bathroom door. He sleep walks."

"I do not." Brandon tossed a throw pillow with his non-foot-holding hand, which his brother skillfully batted away.

"Good night, kids," Justin called, as he and Allie disappeared through the kitchen to the back door.

Finally, *finally*, Brandon looked at Lesa. The hand on her foot tightened, but that was the only acknowledgment she got that he knew he was touching her. "What do you want to do? One more episode? Or are you tired?"

Was there a third option? "Oh, I could go for another episode." She had no idea what had happened during the last one, because every shred of attention she had was on the way his hand on her lower extremity had been making her sex pulse.

"Cool." He clicked the remote to start the show and turned back to the screen.

Lesa's heart would have sunk—he wasn't going to take this any further, was he?—but the erection under her leg felt like it might be a bit harder and longer than it had been before his brother and Allie left them alone.

If only her leg had fingers. Toes didn't count.

Brandon wasn't putting moves on her. He wanted her, that was clear enough, but he wasn't doing anything about it. Maybe his enthusiasm from their after-dinner kiss had been buried by second thoughts. He did always seem to be *thinking*.

Or was he? He definitely had that Southern gentleman thing going on. Was he waiting for her to take the next step?

Well, she could do that. So to speak.

She ever so slowly pulled the foot he was holding just enough so that her leg rubbed over his lap, and then she relaxed back into his hand. She did it again.

His breath caught, and his grip loosened, but he didn't let go. Instead, his thumb caressed the arch of her foot on every return move she made.

She shifted her other leg, trying to relieve some of the pressure between her thighs, but impossibly, the feelings there grew stronger, especially when he pushed his thumb against the sole of her foot.

Could she come, just from getting a foot massage? She never would have imagined it before, but now she was starting to think she was about to find out. It probably had more to do with how much she was aware of his arousal than any connection between her toes and her clit.

His breathing stuttered, and he seemed to quiver with tension. His gorgeous lips were pressed tightly between his teeth, and she wanted to get over there and taste him, find out how much he wanted her. Get him to touch more than her damned foot.

Okay. This was crazy. She had to kiss him before her body went up in a cloud of want. She pulled her foot back and sat up.

Chapter Twelve

Brandon felt Lesa shift again. Her leg, rubbing over his dick, had him holding on to sanity by a thread.

Finding his brother and Allie McGrath in flagrante delicto had saved them from making a hasty lust-fueled mistake earlier and given his good sense a chance to remind him of the reasons that he shouldn't get too close to Lesa. She was here for business, not pleasure, and he had a bad track record of getting in too deep with women with ulterior motives. And in spite of the fact that the beer he'd had with dinner had long since dissipated from his bloodstream, she was a woman and might still be feeling it. Sitting here for the past hour with her foot teasing his crotch, however, had given his libido an opportunity to discount his good sense's objections. She was here for business—but she'd pointed out that, even so, this was the best vacation she'd been on in a long time. Hell, he was still technically on vacation, too. And Lesa wasn't Suzanne. She wasn't here to take advantage of his naïveté and rob his family blind—and humiliate him in the process.

Any concern he had that she was suffering a residual

buzz disappeared in a cloud of lust when she very clearly and soberly asked, "Are we going to get naked sooner? Or later?"

He faced her, her dark eyes reflecting the moving images on the television. Which episode was this? It didn't matter. Holding her gaze, he blindly reached for the remote and turned it off. Now the only light was a glow from the kitchen, backlighting her, making a halo around her.

"How did you do that without looking?" she asked.

"Testosterone. It's a guy thing. We can't type without looking at the keyboard, but we can find keys on any remote control, anywhere, with innate precision."

She laughed, the sound vibrating through her body and into his via the connection between her leg and his groin. "What else can you find in the dark?"

It took him less than a second to reach for her and pull her to him. She came willingly, rising to straddle him, her smooth thighs on either side of his hips. The heat from between her legs had him rising up to meet her, feeling their bodies meet there, even through several layers of fabric. He groaned with the need to strip away the barriers.

She looked down at him, her long hair forming a silky curtain around them. Her lips, when he tilted his head up to meet them, were sweeter than he remembered from any of their kisses so far. Even softer and warmer. He took full advantage of her superior position to coax her into leaning into him, to welcoming him into her mouth where he tasted and stroked and nipped. Every time they kissed, he was sure that there wasn't anything that could be better.

But then she moaned, her fingers digging into his shoulders, returning his kiss with a roll of her hips that stroked him from root to tip and left him barely breathing.

He slid his hands from her luscious hips to her waist then up along her rib cage where he paused, not ready to go farther until he was sure she was ready.

She was ready. She took his hands in hers and brought them to her breasts, squeezing his hands harder over her than he would have ever dared. He felt her nipples through the fabric of her bra and T-shirt, stiff against his palms. He so needed to taste her there, to suck her into his mouth, hear her cry his name.

"Oh, God," she sighed, pushing into his touch, kissing him harder, her hands in his hair now. "More."

He had more. Much more. Releasing her breasts to grab her waist, he moved her to her back on the couch and lay over her, his hips still between her legs, so that he could center himself over her core.

Holding himself above her, he tugged at her top. She helped him, yanking it up to her armpits. He pulled down one cup of her bra and exposed her to his view. Even in the dim light from the kitchen, he could see how dark her nipple was, tight and small.

He slid back and kissed his way down the center of her chest, over the soft curve, finally, finally reaching the center. He moved more slowly now. Learning her textures with his lips, feeling the difference between soft skin and pebbled areola, and eventually, hard tip.

He opened his lips over it and barely pressed them back together.

"Do it," she growled, pulling his hair, squirming beneath him.

So he did. He sucked her into his mouth, swirling his tongue over her nipple, and sliding his fingers over the other.

She immediately cried out, arching beneath him. One of her long legs went over his hip and her pelvis rocked against him.

"*Dios*," she whimpered, clutching at his head. "I'm coming. I'm coming." Her upper leg locked around him, holding him tight to her, and she trembled. The tension in her body telegraphed through every point of contact, and he had to concentrate to keep from following her over the edge.

When she began to relax, he released her breast and turned them slightly until they were on their sides, so he could kiss her through the aftershocks while he continued to touch her. This also brought him into a position where he could press his cock against her more fully. He was so hard with wanting her that he could barely think beyond the next kiss.

She anticipated his need and reached between them, sliding her hand over his erection, stroking him though the fabric of his jeans.

And then she moved to his waistband and began to unbutton his fly, her fingers brushing inside against the head of his cock, nearly sending him over the edge. He slid his hands back up her torso, craving the soft feel of her against his palms.

A light switched on. "I guess we should make more noise when we come in from now on," said a gravelly male voice, and the light switched right back off.

Crap. Grandpa. And Brandon had hands on Lesa's breasts.

"What did you say, Dad? What's going on? What happened to the light?" His father stomped through the kitchen.

Lesa shoved at Brandon's shoulders, pulling her shirt back down.

"Clyde? Why is your dad standing there in the dark?" Mom called.

"Are you all daft?" Grandma asked. "Turn on the damned light."

With a *click* heard round the family, the light came back on.

Brandon met Lesa's eyes and smiled ruefully. "Sorry," he mouthed. Had he lost track of days? He though they weren't coming home until…*shit.* Today was Wednesday.

"Bro." Justin stood behind the rest of them, shaking his head and grinning.

"Justin, you're not helping." Allie tugged his arm. At least someone had some common decency. Not his flesh and blood, who all stood in the doorway, watching Brandon try to figure out how to move from between the legs of the woman beneath him without showing them all just how much they'd interrupted.

• • •

"Mom, Dad, Grandma, Grandpa, I'd like you to meet Lesa Ruiz." Brandon rose to a standing position, pulling Lesa along with him, and stood slightly behind her before his family picked their collective jaws up from the living room floor.

"I'm pleased to meet you." Lesa smiled her most welcoming smile, and reached her hand to the younger Mrs. Morgan.

"The pleasure is all mine," Brandon's mother said, smiling warmly and taking Lesa's hand in her firm, smooth grip. She had questions in her eyes, but she didn't voice them, although from the look she shot Brandon, there would be an inquisition later.

"Ruiz," Grandpa mused, stroking his chin. "I remember a Carlos Ruiz."

"Yes, sir. That's my papa."

"How is the old cactus cooker?" the old man asked.

"He's…fine, thank you." Of course, that depended on how you defined "fine." Alive and breathing? Yes. He was fine. Loving his life and living it to the fullest? Not so much.

"Ruiz?" asked Brandon's dad. "The Little Possum Tequila Ruiz?"

"Pequeño Zarigüeya. That's us," Lesa confirmed. Hadn't

he told them he was bringing a guest home? Maybe he hadn't been as specific as he should have been.

Brandon cleared his throat. "Lesa's come to visit Blue Mountain to help her father decide about making a deal with us for our used barrels."

There was silence for a moment while she figured everyone digested the idea of a business associate being discovered under their son with her shirt around her neck.

Then, "Well. That's quite some negotiating you were doing there." Grandpa snickered.

Brandon put his hand on Lesa's shoulder, as though protecting her from the possibility of censure, and continued along as though Grandpa hadn't spoken. "We'll be touring the plant as soon as the still is repaired. In the meantime, we've been sightseeing."

"Is that what you kids are calling it these days? Ow!" Brandon's grandfather grabbed his shoulder where his wife smacked it.

Lesa fought a grin.

Brandon's mother took the opportunity to turn to the rest of the group and make a shooing motion. "Can we please get the rest of the luggage inside? I don't know about the rest of you, but I could use a shower and my own bed right about now." She turned back and nodded to Lesa. "We'll get acquainted over breakfast."

Was that a promise or a threat?

"Glad you're all home safe," Brandon said, releasing Lesa to hug his mom and then Grandma. Aw, geez. There went those warm fuzzies again, cooing and wiggling. He'd only been away from his family for a couple of days. That closeness was something Lesa didn't have with her own family.

She watched his strong shoulders as he shook hands with his father. She was pretty sure he wasn't prone to getting caught making out on the couch like a teenager, but he'd handled the embarrassing situation with a cool head.

"You go on ahead," Grandpa said as the rest of the group filed back into the kitchen. "Justin, put our stuff next to the bed. Grandma will unpack in the morning. I'm going to find out how Brandon got so cozy with Señorita Ruiz here."

And the old man sat down in the recliner and pulled the handle so that the footrest popped up. He crossed his arms over his chest and stared at Brandon and her.

"That is none of your business," Grandma said. "If you don't get downstairs and unpack your grungy underdrawers in the next three minutes, you'll be washing them out by hand all by yourself."

"Fine," Grandpa grumbled, pulling the footrest back in. "I'd just go to Walmart and buy some new ones," he told Brandon and Lesa as he shuffled past, "but they don't carry 'em sturdy enough to hold my junk secure."

"Aw, geez, Grandpa!" Brandon's composure finally cracked. "Really?"

"Well, son, you should understand. These sorts of things are hereditary, you know," Grandpa told Lesa with a wink. "In case you haven't already figured it out, we Morgan men are endowed with— Ow!"

Grandma had come back into the room and grabbed him by the ear.

"For chrissakes, woman!"

Between gritted teeth, she growled, "Get your flat butt downstairs. Now."

"Holy crap." Brandon sighed when they were finally alone again. "I'm really sorry about that. I didn't realize they'd be home tonight."

But Lesa was laughing too hard to answer him.

"So, uh, I guess we should get some sleep. Grandma gets up at the crack of dawn every day, and she'll be fixing a big breakfast, since we have company."

He shoved a hand through his already mussed hair, and she admired the line of stomach that was revealed by his untucked shirt.

And then she couldn't help but look down, where evidence of his recent arousal hadn't completely disappeared.

"Well, okay," she said, moving toward him and stroking her fingers across his tight abdomen, wanting to slide inside his shirt and trace that line of hair she'd glimpsed.

He caught his breath and grabbed her hands, leaning toward her, his lips a hair's breadth from hers. "If you touch me like that, we'll be back to putting on a show for the whole family again, and I don't think I can take any more of Gramps's commentary tonight."

She couldn't resist one tiny glance back down at his crotch. She raised her eyebrows at him, and said, "Well, Gramps certainly has had some interesting information to share. Maybe I'd like to know what else he has to say."

• • •

Thirty minutes later, the family had settled down and all was quiet again. Except for Brandon's libido, which was trying to convince him to sneak into bed with Lesa.

It would be easy enough. The bathroom connected the two rooms. He could just casually go in and accidentally go into his own room, where she was sleeping, on the way out.

He imagined her laying there, also awake, wanting more than one little orgasm. She would welcome him with that sexy smile and scoot over, pulling the covers back to reveal—

He shook his head before he went too far. Because there was a big problem with this idea.

His bed shared a wall with his parents' room. And you could hear everything. Which he knew, because he'd had to listen to his mom and dad do it for the past thirty years.

He had no inclination to make them listen to him have sex, and besides…they'd realize he'd been able to hear them, and wow. The level of awkwardness would be off the scale.

Well, that train of thought had helped settle things a little. What he should be thinking about was how to make sure Lesa was so impressed with Blue Mountain Distilling she'd recommend that her papa sign a deal for their barrels. He reminded himself that, with Mom and Dad home, he'd have to let his current buyers know their barrel availability was about to be cut down significantly.

"Are you awake?" The voice purred in his ear, and Brandon jumped.

"Sorry," Lesa chuckled softly.

He turned toward the side of the bed where she crouched down next to him. "How did you get in here?"

She pointed toward the door to the adjoining bathroom. "How do you think?"

"I mean—how did you get in here without me noticing?"

"You were sleeping?"

"Nope. I was laying here thinking about visiting you." He laughed softly.

"Scoot over. I'm not staying, but it's chilly out here."

He pulled the covers aside, and she slid in next to him, bringing her warm summer scent with her.

She curled on her side, facing him, almost nose to nose on his pillow.

"Hi."

"What's new?" he asked her.

"I just missed you."

"Ah." He nodded, trying to think of something clever to say, but all the blood in his body was pumping into his cock, not his brain.

"Isn't this what people do when they have friends over to spend the night? Crawl under the covers and talk after the parents go to bed?"

"My friends and I usually slept in sleeping bags in the basement," Brandon admitted. "We didn't sleep in the same bed. Maybe that's a girl thing."

"Yes, I suppose. Though the sad story is that my mama was sick so much when I was that age that I didn't get a chance to know any girls well enough to have sleepovers."

"And yet you know me well enough for a slumber party? I'm honored."

"Yes. I think I do." She leaned away and peered at him through the darkness. "So. Know any good ghost stories?" she asked.

"No, but Justin always swore there was a troll under his bed. You'd probably better come closer and protect me."

She giggled and wrapped her upper arm around him, twining her feet with his.

Sexual tension hummed through him, along with something deeper, more desirable. Satisfaction that had nothing—or very little—to do with the blood surging into his cock. The pleasure of having a woman—this woman—that he liked so much, here in the darkness with him, to share confidences under the covers.

"I feel like a bad girl," Lesa said. "Are we going to get in trouble if I'm caught in here?"

"I don't know. But I can spank you if you want," Brandon murmured, the vision of her round, firm backside bent over his lap making his voice hoarser than he intended and sending a surge of lust through him.

He pulled her closer, wanting to feel her press against him, just for a minute. *Oh, Jesus.* Her nipples brushed his chest, and her lips were now millimeters from his. The urge to take her, here, now, to press her back against the pillow and consume her was so powerful he was shaking with it.

Brandon pulled the last shred of sense from somewhere

deep beneath his arousal and said, "We can't do this here."

"I know, but…" She squirmed, and his restraint frayed.

He threw it out there then. No more pretending this was all business anymore. He was in it, just as Lesa had indicated she was. "Darlin,' when we make love, it's gonna require some serious soundproofing."

"Oh." She laughed softly and nipped at his lips, eliciting a groan that he barely muffled.

"This place is built to withstand a nuclear bomb from the outside, but unfortunately, the walls are paper thin. I've been meaning to get my own house put up one of these days, but situations like this don't arise all that often." He'd hoped he'd have a wife—or at least a fiancée—to help him plan it. If it was left up to him alone, a house would have nothing more than four walls, a bedroom, kitchen, and living room. He'd rather his future house be built for some bigger purpose— like entertaining and raising a family, and that house had all kinds of pretty junk in it. So he hadn't done it yet.

Lesa's hand was stroking his side, fingers feathering over his ribs and hip and back up again, making it hard to think. So to speak.

But there was more than the noise involved that prevented him from making love to Lesa Ruiz at this particular moment. And he needed to say it. Because in spite of his previous mistakes, and his resolution to never, ever again get romantically involved with someone he was working with, he was doing it. And while it seemed that the sexual part of this equation was inevitable, the tragic ending didn't have to be.

"Lesa, I—" He cleared his throat. "I'm more attracted to you than I ever thought was humanly possible." And that was an understatement. "But—"

"Oh, no. Not a 'but'. Unless it's yours." She gave him a firm squeeze.

This time his groan wasn't muffled, and he heard Maude

whine from the hallway in response.

"You're killing me here." He found the self-control to grab her hand and hold it, though his fingers laced with hers. "I've made bad decisions before when I was involved with someone I did business with. I don't want to mess this up. Either this"—he waved between them—"or the possibility of doing business with Little Possum."

She stilled for a moment, then said, "I get it. The good news is, we're not *involved*, because, as you know, my life plan is to be a nomad, so I won't be hanging around. As soon as the ink is even *wet* on an agreement between you and my father, I'm out of here."

A zing of disappointment shredded his mood. But he knew this. She'd told him earlier she wanted to travel and write books about her journeys and the liquors of the world. This would be a fling. Nothing more, so he pushed his hurt feelings aside.

She hesitated, seemed to withdraw for a moment, then said, "I'm going to strongly recommend to my father that I am endorsing Blue Mountain. It's a solid company."

"But you haven't seen it all. There are still things that—"

"Shh. You are an honorable businessman. You will be an ideal collaborator. The people who work for you admire you, and you follow through on your promises. I don't care what problems you have in the plant. Blue Mountain is a good company."

Lesa had pulled her hand free of his while she'd spoken and now rested it along his jaw. Her soft touch warmed him inside and out. Such faith. It was the kind of belief he'd spent the last five years working to build in his family, and she gave it so freely.

"I'm going to go back to my own side of the bathroom before your mama comes in," Lesa whispered into his neck, sending a shiver over Brandon's skin that had nothing to do with tickles. "Maybe tomorrow we should go somewhere… away. Far into the woods. Where your family won't interrupt us."

"Hmmm." He mused. They were going to go somewhere alone, all right, but he was damned if he would end up with mosquito bites or poison ivy or bear claw marks down his back. He knew just the place.

Chapter Thirteen

Lesa ran fingers through her still-wet hair and shivered in the morning mist that blanketed the Blue Mountain valley. What passed as winter clothing in Mexico didn't work for spring wear in Kentucky. Her new Horse Park sweatshirt was in the wash, so Brandon had given her a Blue Mountain Bourbon hoodie, which she snuggled into now and watched the sunrise from her perch in a rocking chair on the front porch.

It was so beautiful and peaceful here. Even though the cars whizzing by on the main thoroughfare just a half mile away went to big jobs at factories and offices in nearby Lexington, there was something about the way the sun shone on the dew here that made her feel like she was years away from the modern world.

Here, she felt like she was staying in the interesting story, and she was a part of it.

Weird.

The door from the house creaked open, and two brown, snuffling forms darted out, wagged in a circle around Lesa, and clambered down the steps to the yard to do their things.

"You like it black and sweet, right?" A steaming cup of coffee appeared next to her, attached to the sturdy forearm of the man she was beginning to feel like she'd known forever.

Very unsettling. Lesa had to search for the grip of the claustrophobia that usually surrounded her when she got too close to someone. It was there, crouched in the corner, like an old frenemy.

"Good morning," Brandon said as she took the coffee, and he came around her to take his place in another rocking chair. The seats were worn and creaky, but sturdy, as though they'd been designed to hold the backsides of many people before and after their current occupants. "Are you up for a little road trip today?"

"Always," Lesa said, but then realized that while she was interested in going anywhere Brandon wanted to take her, she'd be just as happy staying here on this porch.

For a while. She reminded herself that she wasn't planning to stick around. Was her plan to spend a week or so with the sexy son of a distiller about to backfire on her? She couldn't afford to get stuck on him. She'd made a decision, though, while cuddled up to him in bed last night. She was going to tell Papa to take the deal. He wouldn't be able to afford it very easily, but the barrel deal with Blue Mountain would be successful, and she'd be willing to stick around a little longer to make sure he was okay. It wouldn't be long before the tequila would be ready to go to market and Papa would be making money again.

She took a sip of her coffee and looked at Brandon. "Where are we going?"

"It's a surprise."

Something warm slid through her. He cared enough to plan a surprise for her. And she liked it. *Bad. Very bad.* "I should tell you that I don't like surprises."

After a brief flash of uncertainty, his face cleared, eyes

narrowed. "Nuh uh. You're not going to get me to tell you."

"But how do I know what to wear? What should I bring with me?"

"Wear what you've got on. Bring a change of clothes just like it."

A frisson of pleasure spread from her head to her feet. They were going to spend the night together. Yes. She jumped to her feet, her coffee and the peaceful morning forgotten. "When are we leaving? I should go get my things together."

Brandon laughed. "Okay, Miss Hates Surprises. We'll leave as soon as I talk to my dad for a few minutes and you get gathered up."

She grabbed her mug and headed inside, waving good morning to Brandon's dad, who was making his own coffee as she passed through the kitchen.

She'd take another pair of jeans and some shorts, just in case. And she had those silky lavender pajamas, in the event she needed them. She hoped she wouldn't need them. But what if they were camping, like she'd suggested last night? She should bring a sweatshirt if they were going to be sleeping outside somewhere.

Turning, she headed back toward the kitchen to ask, but stopped when she heard Brandon speaking to his father.

"I just hope I'm not making a mistake," he was saying.

Was he talking about her?

"Son, you've got to get over this. You missed a few signs once, and it bit you—bit all of us—in the ass. But that was a long time ago. You're older and wiser now, and you've got better sense than all the rest of us put together when it comes to making wise choices for this business."

There was silence for a moment, and Lesa knew she should turn back around and retreat. She shouldn't be listening to a private conversation, but she also couldn't seem to make herself leave. What had happened before that was so terrible?

"Okay. I think this is a good thing, this deal. And I'm pretty sure I've got the agreement set up so that we can't get our asses handed to us."

His dad laughed. "It's okay to take a few risks."

"Maybe for you." There was a rustle of papers. "Do me a favor and read over this offer I wrote up for Carlos Ruiz. If you're okay with it, go ahead and send it."

Lesa grinned to herself and headed back down the hall, questions about pajamas forgotten. Brandon trusted what she'd told him, that she was going to get Papa to do business with him. That made her feel like she'd accomplished something great. And she had. She was fulfilling her promise to her mama by helping Papa and making Brandon a good deal, too. For some reason, it felt even better to know that she was doing good business with Brandon. Now she just had to convince Papa to behave.

"*Hola*, Papa," Lesa said, shaking her head at Brandon, who motioned from inside of the McDonald's where they'd stopped for lunch. No, she didn't want to Super Size her Diet Coke. While Brandon turned and got in line for food, Lesa checked in with her father.

"How are things?" she asked him.

"What are you learning about Blue Mountain Bourbon?" Papa asked without answering her question.

"This is a good company," she told him. "The employees are happy, and everyone works hard. The product is well regarded in the area, and with so much competition, that seems like a very good sign as well." She omitted her plans to be naked with the owner's son in the next several hours.

"Hmph."

"You're not pleased?"

"Of course, of course. So is the building repaired yet?"

"Well, not quite. The repairs to the damaged rickhouse might take a few months, but they seem to have things on track."

"Oh." His distrust came through the line. "Is everything else working as it should?"

"Yes, Papa. Let's do this."

There was silence on the other end.

"Papa?"

"I'll think about it."

"I hope so," Lesa said, telling Papa that she'd talk to him again in a couple of days. He wasn't telling her something. But then, there was a lot that she wasn't telling him, too.

She pocketed her phone and smiled at Brandon. It must have worked, because he shouldered open the door and smiled back at her. Heat flared inside her. They were going to do this. They were going to be together, alone soon, hopefully somewhere with a mattress.

"How's your dad?" he asked.

"Okay. Wants to know how things are here."

"What did you tell him?"

"I said everything's fine."

"For as much as you've paid attention," he teased. "You've done more sightseeing than distillery-seeing."

She laughed. "Yeah, well, I have excellent instincts, and my instincts tell me that you're a good risk."

"Good. He should have the proposal for a contract in a few hours."

"Great," she said. Her goal of having PZ in shape and herself off the hook was closer by the minute.

"So I'm going to suggest an agreement for a partial shipment of goods—"

She held up her hand. "I don't need the details. They'll go in one brain cell and out the other. I'm still on vacation."

"Fine."

"Are you pouting? I just think that we both—you especially—need to put work away for a while. Let's have some more holiday."

He shook his head. "I don't understand why anyone would want to do that, but for you, I'll try. Here you go," he said, and reached a big hand toward her, holding two enormous drink cups.

So much for no Super Sizing. She hoped he didn't mind pulling over to find a restroom every thirty minutes until they got wherever they were going.

He must have had a psychic inspiration, because he said, "Don't worry. There's enough salt on the gigantic orders of fries to soak up all the pop. You should be able to make it to the next rest area."

"Great," she grumbled good-naturedly. "And my blood pressure and my fingers will be super sized, too."

"Perfect," he said. "Sausage fingers will be incredibly appealing to the fishies."

"Fish? We're going fishing?" She thought about what he said. "With our fingers? Oh, no, señor studmuffin. I don't care how cute you are. I'm not about to stick my hand in the mud to spaghetti for catfish."

Brandon laughed so hard that he had to put his drink and bag of food on the hood of his car and clutch his belly.

"What's so funny?"

"It's—it's called noodling," he gasped. "Not spaghetti-ing."

"Oh. Well, I don't care what it's called. I'm not gonna do it."

He grabbed her around the waist then and smacked a big kiss on her lips. Grinning down at her, he said, "Don't worry. No noodling. No fishing at all. I promise."

"Oh. Then what are you talking about?" she asked, as she

pulled her door open and set her drink in the cup holder. "No, Mabel," she told the dog, shoving her nose back. "You don't get any."

Maude whined from behind Brandon's seat, no doubt smelling the luscious, greasy food.

"Hold on, girls. I got you Happy Meals, like I promised," he said. To Lesa, he said, "Still not gonna tell you where we're going. You're going to have to suck it up and wait."

She sighed, shoving her seat belt into the fastener. "Fine. But we better get there before this six-liter drink gets through my system."

"No worries," Brandon said, pulling into traffic behind a hot pink and chrome speedboat that was long enough to require its own zip code.

Well, she thought, diving into her Big Mac. Whatever they were doing, hopefully it would keep her mind off of Papa and his financial troubles. Her previous good feelings about making this trip successful were a little shaky, after hearing Papa's voice and his reluctance to listen to her opinion, but she was determined to spend the next however many hours with Brandon enjoying his company and not worrying about the future. It would get there soon enough. It always did.

The landscape had changed as they'd driven down Interstate 75. The rolling hills strung with white or black fences interspersed with wooded hills had given way to bigger hills covered with forests, now interspersed by stretches of small farms, tin-roofed schools, and the occasional trailer home. They left the main highway at McDonald's and sped along a two-lane state route with few major intersections.

The road began to wind higher and higher and then descend.

A couple of times Lesa feared they were about to tumble over the edge of the road into the trees. Mixed with the fact that, for some reason, she was beginning to feel nervous about being alone with Brandon. She'd flirted and teased and played with him, but this felt more…real. Her "I'm on vacation and I'm going to have a fling" attitude was shifting somehow, and she wasn't sure she liked it.

"The roads here are as scary as Mexico," she observed. "How do people with boats do this?" She grabbed the dashboard as Brandon swung around a curve and hit his brakes to avoid driving up the back end of one of the boats in question. "And why are there so many boats in the mountains, anyway?"

"Hold on for two more seconds," Brandon told her.

Mabel and Maude, who'd been hanging their heads out of the rear window, sending strings of drool along the back of the car the whole drive, began to shuffle and whimper with excitement, occasionally bringing a head back inside to bark in Brandon's direction.

"It's okay, girls. I know. We're almost there," he told them. "Aaaand…here you go."

He swung the SUV around one last bend in the road and the forest opened to reveal an immense stretch of water, sparkling for miles in the distance, sending tendrils between wedges of stone and forested fingers of land.

"Oh…" It was breathtaking. Just ahead of them, the road ended in a gravel parking lot and boat ramp, a marina teeming with activity. Colorful boats of all shapes and sizes bobbed at their moorings next to covered docks, and other boats drifted in and out of the area, making use of the marina's services.

"What is this?" Lesa asked.

"This," Brandon told her, pulling into a parking slot and shoving the vehicle in park, "is Lake Cumberland. I heard a rumor that the marina had de-winterized the Blue Mountain family houseboat, so I thought maybe we should stop down and make sure it still runs."

So they were on a family holiday, just without the family.

A shiver of anxiety ran over Lesa's skin, which was weird, because she was here to have a sexy few days with a handsome guy who was just as into her as she was into him.

Shaking off the unease, she thought about what she'd packed. What Brandon had told her to pack, and not to pack. *Oh, no*. "There is a big problem with your plans," Lesa told him.

"What's that?"

"I didn't bring a swimsuit."

Brandon wiggled his eyebrows at her. "*Is* that a problem?"

Chapter Fourteen

"No, really. I was kidding. Sort of." Brandon followed Lesa through the marina store while she sorted through the bathing suit options. "I figured that one of the girls would have left a suit. Oh. That would work," he said, to the barely-existing scraps of fluorescent pink fabric she held up.

"I don't think so." She thrust the suit back onto the rack with a scowl.

The next one was a high-necked tank suit.

"No." He shook his head.

She checked the tag. "It's my size, and the price is right."

"Aw, Lesa, come on," he begged. He was sorry. He really hadn't considered that she'd need a suit. There were always a dozen or more swimsuits in the houseboat. Except this year, because Lorena had been the last person to stay there last year, and she'd done a better than average job of cleaning when she'd vacated the premises.

And Lesa was mad at him.

He followed her to the cash register, docile as could be, though he did grab a bag of Cheetos and a six-pack of bottled water on the way. After a glance at Lesa's set chin, he added a four-pack of Reese's Cups to toss onto the counter next to her Victorian nanny swim suit. He didn't dare comment, lest she decide she wasn't going to come out in the sun at all.

"You want anything special, snack-wise?" he dared to ask. "I picked up some extra stuff when we stopped at the grocery store in town, but if there's something…" He hoped the chocolate would soothe her pique, but maybe she had different preferences from his mom and the McGrath girls.

"No thank you," she said, formally.

"I've got that," Brandon told Margie, the middle-aged lady who'd worked there for as long as he could remember. "Just put it all on my bill."

Lesa turned and scowled at him. "You don't have to buy this for me," she said.

"Uh, yeah. I think I do. That way it's mine, and I can burn it after you don't need it anymore," he said, eyeing the monstrosity. Chances were, it would be too cold to get in the water today, anyway, and they'd just spend the afternoon sitting in the sun on the top deck of the houseboat. She could get away with shorts and a tank top if she wanted. But after she realized that he meant them to spend the day on the water, and that she didn't have a swimsuit to wear, she'd gotten grumpy.

Hence his attempt at conciliatory chocolate.

Margie smiled sympathetically at Brandon as she stuffed the purchases into a couple of bags.

"It may not be summer, but the sun's still pretty strong," she said. "Do you need any sunscreen?"

"No, there's still enough of that on the boat from last year," he grumbled.

Lesa cut her gaze at him, and he thought he caught a flash of humor.

Was she playing him? That would be fine. He was open

to tormenting. She didn't need to go to extremes to tease him, though. Picking a high-necked, flannel swimsuit was taking things too far.

Okay. It wasn't really flannel. But still.

He followed Lesa from the marina store to the wooden walkway. Maude and Mabel paced and whined from the deck of the "Ship and a Bottle," anxious to get underway.

The family boat was moored on the second dock away from the marina, so it only took a few silent moments to reach their slot and toss their purchases onto the picnic table on the AstroTurf-covered platform at the back of the boat.

"What do you need me to do?" Lesa finally spoke, her annoyance with him apparently stashed for the moment.

"Margie says they've got us all ready to go, so we just need to get untied."

"Should I change first or wait until we're underway?" she asked.

"Whatever you like." That was neutral. His personal opinion was that the granny suit she'd bought should find its way to the bottom of the lake, but he was keeping that to himself.

Then he mentally smacked himself in the head for being an asshole. He didn't need to see Lesa in a string bikini to know that he was over-the-moon hot for her. She could probably wear sackcloth and ashes and he'd be unable to keep his eyes off of her.

He was just frustrated that she'd gotten so mad at him for not giving her a heads-up about the suit.

"Well, let's get out on the water so these dogs can stop pacing," she said, hopping along the edge of the boat to the front and leaning over the railing to reach for the rope holding the side to the cleat.

Brandon shrugged and went inside, checking the gauges to confirm that the gas tank was full, and that the battery was charged. All was good. He turned the key, and the diesel engine roared to life, then rumbled happily, waiting to shift into gear.

He checked to see that Lesa had gotten all of the ropes untied.

"Okay, we're ready. Keep your arms and legs inside the ride at all times!" he called out. Checking to make sure that there were no other boats passing behind them, he threw the boat into gear and began to back out, into the mainstream of the marina. He took a deep breath. It was boat season. Everything was in its place. The dogs on the deck—Maude and Mabel now, but there had been several family dogs before his pair of hounds. There was beer in the cooler, hamburgers in the fridge to toss on the gas grill later. When they got back the marina, there was always ice cream from the store.

As the houseboat was shifted into forward and began to move toward the open water of Lake Cumberland, Lesa turned from the front deck and smiled at Brandon.

Good. Maybe he was forgiven. Hopefully. He really wanted to share his love of the lake with her.

She stepped through the open door to the main cabin where he stood at the wheel and said, "I'll change now, okay?"

"Sure," he told her. "We're gonna go up to the next cove for now and tie up for a while. The dogs like to swim, and they'll start whining if we don't give them a chance to wear themselves out as soon as possible."

"*Start* whining?" She laughed and shoved a whimpering Mabel out of her way to one of the staterooms.

The smells of diesel exhaust and lake water were like a balm to his soul. The first boat ride of the season always made Brandon feel like he'd been holding his breath the rest of the year.

He reached above him to the ancient CD player and pushed play.

The melodic drumbeat opening to the Talking Heads' *Psycho Killer* thumped throughout the floating camper. As David Byrne began to sing, Mabel and Maude came to sit on Brandon's feet. The three of them began to participate in houseboat karaoke.

They'd just begun to rock it out, "Oh, oh oh ohhhhh…ai yi yi yi yi yiiii…" when Lesa reappeared.

Covered from shoulder to knee in Dad's 2XL Cincinnati Bengals T-shirt. And peeking out from below that, her legs were covered to ankle in a towel.

He grinned. She could torment him all she wanted, but she was hot. And from the wry twist to her luscious lips, she knew it.

Reaching up to turn the music down, he tried to shush the dogs, but they weren't quite done singing along.

"Are we there yet?" Lesa shouted over the joyful howls and barks.

"Almost." Brandon slowed the big boat and began the turn into his favorite secluded cove. There were so many twists and turns in this lake—this one appeared to be a short, blind cove, but just as you thought the boat would crash into the stone wall at the end, another turn was revealed, allowing the houseboat room to maneuver and remain hidden from the main lake.

"This is so beautiful," Lesa said, rubbing the finally quiet Maude's ears. "And huge."

"There's enough water in this lake to cover all of Kentucky with three inches of water."

"Really." She looked over the railing. "That's a lot of water."

"Yup. There are supposedly a bunch of towns at the bottom of the lake that got flooded when they built the dam."

"Oooh. I wonder if the ghosts ever swim up and grab people?"

Oh, hell. That was one of his childhood nightmares. "We all wear life jackets in the water. That way they can't pull you all the way under." At least he hoped not. Judging that they were close enough to shore, he cut the engine.

He opened a locker on the deck, pulled out a rope and tossed it over a low-hanging tree limb. He'd have to go in and grab the other end to tie the boat off, but he had a few minutes before they drifted too far.

"Come on, Maude. Mabel." He pulled out the custom doggie life jackets his mother insisted on and snapped an excited Maude into one.

Lesa took the other and got to work on her sister.

"Okay, just a sec." He found his own life jacket. This was gonna suck. It was still early spring, and even though the day was hot and sunny, the water would be icy. There would be shrinkage. Major shrinkage. But there was nothing for it.

He opened the gate from the deck and turned to look at Lesa. "I'm doing this for you," he said, and with his best Tarzan yell, jumped, feet first, into the frigid lake water.

He heard the dogs hit the water behind him as he surfaced and began to stroke toward the shore. Reaching the rocks at the water's edge, he carefully pulled himself up and grabbed the loose end of the rope. A few good knots, and the boat would be secure for as long as they wanted to stay here.

He turned to see Lesa watching him from the deck.

"Are you gonna come out in the sunshine? After you invested in that lovely swimsuit, it would be a shame if you sat there covered up all day," he called.

"Well," she said, dropping the towel, and reaching for the hem of the T-shirt. "Turns out that suit didn't fit after all." And without another word, she pulled the T-shirt over her head to reveal—her. Stark, raving naked.

All of the air went out of Brandon's lungs, and the shrinkage he'd worried about from the cold water was completely, throbbingly, reversed.

She was exquisite, as he'd known she would be. Softly rounded in all the right places. He couldn't decide what to look at first...those amazing breasts...the dark triangle at the apex of her thighs...slender waist...glorious legs...

Before he could figure it out, she'd buckled a float around her waist and ran full speed off the edge of the boat.

• • •

Damn, the water was *cold*. There were dogs circling Lesa, trying to climb her while she treaded water.

It had been totally worth it to see the look on Brandon's face when she'd revealed herself to him, though. She'd really had him going, thinking she was mad at him and then pretending to want to wear the granny suit in the sun.

The heat in his eyes cut through the chill in the water as he made his way back over the rocks to the water's edge and let himself down into the lake.

As he stroked his way through the water toward her, she shoved at the dogs. Seeing their master in the water distracted them enough to leave her, and he said something to them, threw a stick he'd grabbed from the shore back up on the rocks, and the dogs went after it.

"Hi," he said, when he was within a couple of feet of her position.

"Hi," she said back.

His wet hair was pushed back from his high forehead, and he looked younger, more innocent. Like she imagined he'd been as an earnest teenager. The sun glinted on his pale gold skin.

"Are you cold?" He looked down at her breasts, which bobbed at the water's surface, nipples beaded harder than she thought they'd ever been.

"Yeah, but I'm glad to see you, too." She looked at him with all the want she'd been storing up for the days—weeks—years she'd known him. Because even though she hadn't met him all that long ago, she'd let him get closer to her, to see more of her—inside—than she'd ever shown anyone else.

He grinned and swam a little closer. "I'm glad to see you, too. So to speak."

She looked down, through the clear lake water to where Brandon's legs treaded through the water, but the ripples made it difficult to see how glad he was.

Teeth chattering, he laughed and said, "It might be June before my boys come back out of my body cavity to say hello, though."

She was cold, but his lips were blue, Lesa realized. Even though he'd gone onto shore for a few moments, he'd been wet longer than she had. "Let's get out of this water." She turned and paddled back toward the boat, and the ladder that hung from the side.

She reached it first, and hung on to the rope, motioning for him to hurry. "Come on. Let's get you warmed up."

"You go up the ladder first. That ought to get my furnace cranking." He reached her side and floated into her with a well-aimed kiss. His lips were not hot.

"No! Get in. Now." She shoved him in front of her and followed him up the ladder, coming onto the deck immediately behind him and grabbing the towel she'd dropped before her skinny dip.

He shed his life jacket as he turned and reached to unbuckle her float belt. She snapped the towel open behind her and wrapped their bodies in a cold, damp cocoon of terry cloth.

His body warmed immediately against her bare front and seemed to be recovering from the cold quite well, based on the way the front of his swim trunks jabbed her in the belly.

"I need to lose these wet pants," he murmured against her. "Skin to skin is a more effective way to share body heat."

He wriggled and she felt the wet trunks hit the tops of her feet as he stepped out of them.

And they were naked. Finally. At last. Suddenly, overwhelmingly pressed against each other.

Lesa was suddenly shivering more than Brandon had been a moment before, but it wasn't because she was cold. Everywhere her body touched his burned and was only soothed by more touching.

His breath stuttered out of his chest when he lowered his mouth to hers, pressing his lips against hers, seeking entrance, nipping and licking.

She kissed him back, inhaling his breath, holding his wet body against her. Every hair on his body stroked her smooth skin, sensitizing her, every nerve ending firing in want for his touch.

His hands slid over her hips, pulling her even closer to him. Her fingers were tangled in the towel so she couldn't touch him, but her breasts rubbed against his chest, nipples rasping in the coarse hair over his pecs, aching, sending pulses between her legs. She leaned even closer, until he finally, finally moved those hands higher and cupped each breast — both soothing the need and building it higher.

His erection nestled into her belly, and her sex ached to feel him inside of her.

"I want you," he growled into her ear, the vibrations running along the side of her neck and down her spine to make her thighs clench.

She might have whimpered, her knees definitely gave slightly, but he held her tight, like he might never let her go. A drop of sanity intruded, and she wondered, "Should we go inside?"

"Yeah. Yeah, we should." He loosened his hold on her —

just as the boat began to rock. "What the —"

Lesa lost her balance and Brandon caught her against him as Mabel or Maude, she wasn't sure, clambered aboard the boat. The other dog followed, making the boat tip back and forth even more.

The girls wound themselves between Lesa and Brandon's legs, shaking and soaking their nearly dry bodies.

"Argh!" Brandon shoved the dogs away, and Lesa rewrapped the towel around herself, laughing in spite of the frustration coursing through her body.

"Maude, shoo. I never should have shown you how to use the damned ladder," he cursed, shutting the gate then unbuckling the dogs' life vests.

He turned his head to look up at Lesa. "One thing I can tell you. These dogs are going to take a long, long nap now. I bet if you went and got the shower warmed up, I could guarantee that we'll be alone for at least the next hour or two."

"That's something I can do," she agreed and dropped the towel, padding through the living room of the houseboat.

"Jesus, woman," she heard Brandon curse behind her. "You're gonna give me a heart attack if you keep walking around like that."

Chapter Fifteen

Brandon locked the sliding door behind him, sequestering the dogs on the deck of the boat. He grabbed a condom from the small duffel bag of overnight things he'd packed and went down the short hallway to the tiny bathroom. He paused for a moment to appreciate Lesa's silhouette through the frosted glass of the shower enclosure.

She stood in profile, back arched, hands in her glorious dark hair. Her figure was all curves and energy, never completely still, and pulling him forward with a force that he couldn't resist.

She wasn't his forever woman. But for now, she was here, and she wanted him.

His body throbbed in response to her presence, every muscle primed to claim her.

Reaching behind to pull the door shut, she startled him by opening the shower door and sticking her head out.

"Why are you locking the door? We're alone here, right?"

"I'm not taking any chances. The way things between us keep getting interrupted, the girls might sprout opposable thumbs before we seal this deal."

Her throaty laugh made his cock twitch.

She noticed, and her eyes darkened, focused on him. Pushing the door of the shower open, she said, "Get in here."

And still he paused.

"What are you waiting for?"

"I—" He was such a sap. He'd been at least half-hard for this woman since he'd met her, and he just wanted to stand there and look at her smiling at him with water streaming over her shoulders onto her luscious curves. He wanted to preserve this moment to remember later, when she'd left, and his life had gone back to its normal, boring existence. Since when had he thought his regular life was boring? Since he'd met Lesa Ruiz.

"You're so damned beautiful," was all he finally said.

With a laugh, she rolled her eyes and stepped back into the steam, so he followed her.

As soon as he got the door closed behind him, he bent his head to rinse the lake water from his hair—then immediately bashed his skull against the showerhead, because Lesa had knelt and taken him in her mouth.

"Fuuuuck," he groaned, feeling her silky tongue slide across the head, her hand wrapped around his shaft.

He couldn't look away when he met her eyes—crinkled at the edges with a smile—and she wrapped her lips around him and pulled him in, stroking him with her tongue. He threaded his fingers through her hair as his arousal went from already off-the-charts to never-before-in-this-lifetime. The warm water pouring over his body and her hot, wet mouth were the most exquisite feeling he knew and very shortly had his balls drawing up and legs tensing.

"Lesa, stop," he begged, tugging her head back.

She leaned away, staring up at him. "No?"

Jesus. Her mouth was open and wet, swollen. For him.

His dick arched between them, aching and yearning.

"Oh, yes. But I need to touch you. I don't want this to be over yet."

She quirked a smile. "There's no law that says you can't come first."

"Yeah there is. It's the I'm-likely-to pass-out-from-pleasure law. And I'm nothing if not an equal opportunity lover," he told her, urging her to her feet.

"Oh yeah?" She stood, moving as far away from him as the narrow space allowed.

"Yeah." He followed, leaning over her, finally, finally in a position to touch her as much as he wanted. Everything he wanted to kiss and lick was right here. Right now. Her moan echoed around him as he pulled her nipple into his mouth and sucked, tugging a moan from her that caressed his balls. He needed to focus on her, but every touch, every squeeze made his own need that much stronger.

He slid a hand along the inside of her thigh, higher, to find her slick and ready for him. So wet, so smooth. Her fingers threaded through his hair as he parted her folds and traced her opening, spreading slippery arousal over her flesh.

"Aaaah," she cried out, when his thumb brushed the firm knot of her clit, and her knees buckled.

Releasing her breast, he supported her with an arm around her waist and kissed her mouth again, tangling his tongue with hers, thrusting against her lips as he strummed between her legs. This close together, her face was fuzzy to him, so he stopped kissing her long enough to look at her clearly while he touched her. She looked up at him, slightly dazed expression, eyes struggling to stay focused. Orange and lime filled the small space, elusive enough to make him want to chase the source with his whole being.

Lesa's hair stuck to her shoulders and the shower wall as she tossed her head back and forth, legs tightening around his hand. She gripped his shoulders and held on to him while she rose on her toes.

His erection pressed against her hip, begging him to enter her, so he tried to keep his rhythm while doing mental math.

Clenching around his fingers tighter and tighter, she whimpered and moaned as her arousal climbed. Her orgasm, when it finally broke, was so beautiful, he nearly lost it.

He watched her chest flush with color and her breathing slow, glorious lips softly parted. She gazed at him, her thoughts unfathomable. Until the side of her mouth quirked, and she straightened. "Turn off the water, *jefe*," she ordered.

He hadn't realized the hot water had run out, and he was once again in danger of being soaked and cold.

No, he wasn't. Because as soon as he'd shut off the tap, she reached for the condom he'd placed in the soap dish.

She tore open the package and began to roll the latex over the head of his straining erection. Her touch pushed his arousal higher, and he jerked.

"Wait, you have to leave some space," he said, shoving her hand away in his hurry to get the job done.

"I want to help," she protested, reaching to steady his shaft.

He groaned at the feel of her hot fingers surrounding him. "You're not helping."

Together, laughing, they managed to get themselves protected and stood, staring at each other. Slowly, Lesa slid one sleek leg along his, raising her knee toward his waist, opening herself to him.

Holding her gaze, he bent his knees and leaned in, reaching to guide himself toward her slippery entrance, finding her own hand there, also trying to help.

They both chuckled, and she lifted her arms. "I surrender," she said.

"Thank God." With one firm push, he was inside her,

surrounded by her heat, feeling her hold him within her body. A perfect fit.

She wrapped her arms around his shoulders and he grabbed her legs, holding her up, and open, and completely at his mercy as he leaned into her and began to thrust.

"Oh, *Dios*," she panted. "Omigod."

Brandon didn't think he'd ever felt so turned on, so energized as he did right this moment. He was both certain he wanted to do this, exactly this, for the rest of his life, and positive that he was going to come any second.

They moved together like it was meant to be, like their bodies were made for this, in this space, in this moment.

"Oh, Brandon. Oh, God," Lesa cried.

He felt her tense around him, and he had to hold on tighter to her legs. Fingernails raked his back while she pulsed around him. Tension coiled at the base of his spine, coalesced in his balls, and sent waves of pleasure through every cell in his body, and he came like he'd never come before.

He might have blacked out for a moment, but when the world reformed around him, he was aware of Lesa stroking his arms, somehow relaxed between him and the shower wall, legs still cradling his hips.

The boat rocked gently, and waves lapped against the pontoons.

"That was nice," she sighed. "When do you think we can do it again?"

"We might have to stay like this," Brandon rasped. "I don't think I can unlock my knees."

• • •

Lesa wasn't sure she could move, either, but the idea of dying in a houseboat bathroom—even with her shriveled body wrapped around Brandon's—was enough to get her moving.

The damned room was *tiny*.

"We should disengage," he said, after a few more seconds.

"Yes." But she took another second to function, because it felt so good to be connected like this. Her physical return to earth was shaky. Still quivering with aftershocks, she pulled herself up against his torso. He let go of her leg, and as she slowly lowered it to the shower floor he slipped from her body. She nearly cried at the loss.

"Are you okay?" he asked, holding her elbow.

"I think so, just don't get too far."

He snorted and looked around the room. "I don't think I can."

True. There was about two cubic inches of extra space.

When she was finally on her own two feet, he disposed of the condom and handed her a dry towel.

He kept one for himself, rubbing at his hair then drying off the rest of his fabulous body. Lesa followed suit, finally wrapping the towel around herself, securing it by tucking one end in under her arm. Such a domestic thing—being handed a towel—and yet it sent a weird zing through her insides, making it hard to breathe. Although it was possible that they'd used up all the oxygen in the bathroom.

When they finally exited the bathroom, the formerly bright day had dimmed, and the dogs were pacing anxiously on the deck.

"Crap. I didn't know it was supposed to rain," he said. "There goes my plan to see if you wanted to sunbathe nekkid on the roof of the boat."

Lesa bent to peer out of the window. "It does look dark out there. Are we safe here?"

"Safer back in here than we'd be out on the open water," he told her. One hand on the sliding door, he asked, "Do you care if I let the girls inside?"

"God, no. They look terrified."

And indeed they were. The minute the door opened enough to admit them, Mabel practically climbed over Maude in her hurry to get in, and both dogs made a beeline for the galley kitchen table, crawling underneath and trying to get as far from "outside" as possible.

"Big babies," he scolded with a gentle smile. He left the door open to admit a heavy breeze, which carried the scent of rain and did little to blow away the claustrophobic feeling Lesa had gotten while in the tiny bathroom. She shook it off and focused on the dogs.

"How long have you had them?" Lesa asked. They were obviously as devoted to him as he was to them.

He snorted. "It feels like forever." He reached for a cooler that he'd brought and motioned for her to follow him outside, onto the deck. They each took a springy patio chair. From the cooler, Brandon produced a couple of wrapped sandwiches and some grapes, which he put on the table between them. He dug around. "I hope you're hungry. I may have overdone it at the IGA."

"And here I thought you left me in the car for so long because you were stocking up on condoms."

He grinned. "That, too."

"Mmmph," Lesa responded, mouth already filled with smoky ham and cheddar.

After she swallowed, she said, "I never had a dog. We were always going to get one, but then something would happen. 'I promise, if you just wait until summer when you're not in school and can train it, we'll get a puppy.' 'I promise, as soon as tourist season is over, or the agave harvest, or until your mother doesn't have cancer anymore…'" Shit. She hadn't meant to bring that up, but it must have been part of the weird mood she found herself in. And the rain. Rain always made her think of Mama and long days of being shut up in the house, taking care of her.

"That really sucks," Brandon said. "I'm sorry."

"Yeah. It sucked. But it's okay. It was a good way to learn not to make promises I wouldn't keep."

"Hmm." He didn't comment, just opened a bottle of water and handed it to her.

She took another bite of sandwich, chasing it with a drink, searching her brain for a way to change the subject from herself. Normally she loved to talk about her future free-wheeling lifestyle, but right now, she was uncomfortable. So she would focus on Brandon. "Tell me why it's so hard for you to take time off of work."

He jerked his head back. "Oh, damn. I haven't checked my phone once since we got here." He reached for it.

"Oh no you don't," she told him, grabbing it before he could get it. Laughing, she shoved it under the cushion of the chair she sat on. "I shouldn't have brought it up, if I'd known you were going to forget you're taking a few days off."

He rubbed his head. "That's odd. I never stop thinking about work." He narrowed his eyes at her. "Are you working some sort of Aztec magic on me?"

"Yes. That's exactly what it is. Now spill. Why are you a workaholic?"

He turned his head and looked through the window. She followed his gaze and saw that dense gray clouds had descended on the cove, and the water was a still, steel-colored sheet of glass.

"I screwed up really badly a few years ago," he said, staring out over the water. "I was really gung ho to prove myself to the company after I graduated from college. My dad had always been so focused on getting my brother into the business, but Justin had no interest, and I was determined to show him how useful I would be. I was gonna be worth two of Justin."

"How did that work out for you?" Lesa asked, after he'd

been silent for a few seconds.

"Pretty well, actually, with one glaring exception. I've got a knack for forecasting and picking which production management changes will give the best results to the bottom line. And I'm the Supreme Overlord of Inventory Management. That sort of thing."

"Wow. A superhero."

"No. Supreme Overlords are always villains. Don't you know anything?"

She lowered her head and looked at him over the top of her sunglasses. "Inventory management? I don't think evil geniuses bother with that sort of thing."

He shrugged. "Okay, I'll give you that."

"I bet your dad was thrilled."

"I was pretty hot stuff," Brandon admitted. "At least for a while. And then I met the cooper's daughter."

"That sounds like a line from a bad joke."

His laugh didn't hold any amusement. "This one doesn't have a good punch line."

"The cooper—the barrel maker?" Lesa clarified, uncertain in her mental translation.

"Yeah. I met Suzanne when she came to a meeting with her dad, who makes some of the best barrels in Kentucky. She seemed…perfect."

Lesa hated her already.

"Everyone said it was like we were made for each other. She got along with my folks, and she worked in a related industry. And I was willing to go to the occasional country club event."

"Eww. Like garden parties and stuff?"

Brandon shrugged. "Well. I didn't like to go to *all* of the same stuff, so I managed to have to work a lot when those things came up."

"Good thinking."

"Yeah. You'd think so, wouldn't you?" He scratched his ear, shifted around a little. "Anyway. She came to visit me at work a lot. I thought that was great. She even volunteered to file reports for me when I was overloaded with paperwork. God. I was so…naive. I thought she was hanging around because she liked me. Turns out she was setting me up. She wasn't just filing paperwork for me. She was rewriting history. To cover up a theft."

"What?"

"Ja— Someone at the distillery was siphoning off the profits—literally—by stealing barrels of whiskey."

"How does someone steal a barrel of whiskey? That's so heavy!"

"At the time, we were aging some of our bourbon off-site. One of our, uh, employees managed to set it up so that only four of five barrels got delivered to the other site. The rest were bottled and sold elsewhere."

"And she was in on it? That's terrible!" Lesa wanted to find the bitch and do terrible, unladylike things to her. "What happened? How did you find out?"

He rubbed his face with both hands, propped his elbows on his knees, and stared at the floor. "I caught her with…with him. The other person from Blue Mountain, who was, um, married. I confronted her, and she just laughed. Told me this other guy was going to leave his wife and marry her."

Lesa growled.

Brandon looked at her with raised eyebrows.

"I don't like this woman." An understatement.

"Thank you. I don't like her very much anymore, either." He grinned, leaned over, and kissed her.

"Did the married asshole leave his wife?"

Brandon tilted his head left and right and said, "Well, yeah, he left his wife, but he didn't marry Suzanne."

"What happened to her?"

"She went back to work for her dad for a while, but after we did an audit and found all that booze was missing, she pointed her fingers at me, then conveniently moved out of state."

"So you were accused?"

"Yeah, but it didn't hold water. My dad and Lorena knew the truth, that the, uh, employee was responsible."

"I hope he got fired and arrested and sent away for a long time."

"Well...he's gone," Brandon confirmed. "Anyway, Blue Mountain lost a lot of money, and I lost a good bit of credibility, because I was the inventory whiz and should have noticed the discrepancies. Instead, I was noticing, um, other things."

"I'm sure that when you told everyone the employee was sleeping with Suzanne, they understood."

"Yeah, no, I didn't share that part."

"What? Why not? Surely not because her ladylike reputation would be destroyed? She should have been arrested, too!"

He shook his head. "Maybe, but things were bad enough here at the time."

Hmph. Lesa never would have let that go. She'd have hunted Suzanne down and dragged her name through the mud.

"Stop frowning." He reached to stroke her forehead. "You're going to get an eyebrow cramp."

There was that weird zing again—the one she'd felt earlier when he'd handed her a towel.

Thunder rumbled ominously in the distance.

Brandon slapped his knees. "Enough pathetic wallowing. That's the end of my sad story. I spent a long time licking my wounds after that," he said. "I didn't go out much. I gained a bunch of weight. I was a mess. Then, without knowing what the other was doing, Allie and Eve each decided that I needed a dog. One Sunday afternoon, I was sitting on the couch with a bag of Doritos, and Allie showed up with a puppy. Five minutes before Eve."

"And they both picked bloodhounds?"

"From the same litter," he confirmed. "My mom got sucked in because they were so cute, and let me keep both of them. Needless to say, I had to start getting out of the house. Hell, I had to get back to work to buy dog food and pay vet bills. And between taking the dogs for regular exercise and cleaning up after them, I got back in shape."

"I'll say," Lesa said, eying his hard body.

"You know," he said, rising and focusing those intense blue eyes on her, "There a few other things that burn calories and build muscle that don't involve putting on my Asics." He wiggled his eyebrows and reached a hand toward her.

Oh, yes. Yes, there were. "What would those things be? Gymnastics? Yoga?"

"Something like that."

And as the afternoon air crackled with lightning, and thunder rumbled across the lake, they made their own storm inside one of the staterooms, and Lesa's aversion to being in tiny spaces on rainy days was, if not erased, then at least very pleasantly—*very* pleasantly—sidetracked.

Chapter Sixteen

The SUV's headlights swept a familiar road sign, and Lesa peered at it as they left one winding country back road for another. The restaurant where they'd eaten dinner had been east of the lake, and now they were…oh, hell, she didn't know where they were.

"Isn't the marina that way?" She pointed the other direction from which they'd turned.

"Yep." Brandon didn't say anything else, just peered ahead into the darkness.

"Um, okay." Not only had she taken the world's most intense post-coital nap that afternoon, and was still a bit groggy, but she was in a slight food coma, and might have missed a few steps, still… "Aren't the dogs going to complain if we don't go back and get them?"

"Are you in a hurry to get to bed? I mean, it has been almost"—he checked the dashboard clock—"six hours since the last time we were naked, but if you're really desperate, I'm sure we can pull off here somewhere…"

She smacked his arm. "Don't tease me. I might take you

up on it." Was she in a hurry to get to bed? With Brandon? Always. *No, no, no*. Not always. But definitely as often as possible while this new, exciting feeling lasted.

"We're going back to the boat in a bit. I just want to show you something first."

"I—"

"Just enjoy the ride."

"Didn't I drive you crazy enough on the way down here to cure you of this insane need to surprise me with wonders of nature?" she asked.

"You'd think so, wouldn't you," he agreed. "'Brrrandon, where are we going? When are we going to get there? Why won't you tell me?'" He did a pretty good imitation of her, she admitted. And she wasn't as annoyed with him as she wanted to be.

Mr. Amiable. He had some kind of friend-spell he cast on everyone. They'd eaten fried fish and potatoes with coleslaw at a local dive, and Brandon had charmed all of the other customers—locals, fishermen, and houseboating families alike. He'd even passed out miniature bottles of Blue Mountain's newest bourbon, Dangerous Dave's Eight Ball, to everyone over the age of twenty-one. Who traveled with samples of booze?

Brandon Morgan, apparently.

It was disturbing to Lesa how much he was growing on her.

Maybe having sex with him hadn't been the greatest idea she'd ever had.

With the other guys she'd been with on her short vacations away from home, she'd spend a few days getting to know them, then if they meshed, spend a few more days together in bed, but after the second orgasm, she was usually looking for a way to say good-bye.

She was—she counted, five? Six?—orgasms into this

relationship, and she didn't have any urge to— Oh, no. A relationship? No way. That was a long-timer's word.

She rolled the window down, needing some air.

Based on his story about the barrel maker's evil daughter, Brandon was someone who had relationships. And when those ended, he was devastated.

Lesa was not that girl. She wasn't the girlfriend type any more than she was a scheming two-timing thief. She wasn't, right? She wasn't planning to *steal* anything. She had already made up her mind to convince Papa to sign the deal with Blue Mountain, and there was no dirt to find here. Her conscience was clear, and soon, very soon, she would be relieved of her obligations to Papa and free to travel the world. She couldn't wait. She was ready. Really.

Her musing was interrupted when the car left the extreme darkness of the forested road for a dimly lit parking lot. "Here we go."

"Are we here?"

"We are, indeed, here," Brandon told Lesa. "And I think we're just in time."

"For what?"

He just looked at her.

"Fine." She huffed. "Let's go see."

There were other cars in the lot, so whatever they were going to see, they weren't the only ones. Here in the dark. In the middle of an ancient forest in God-Only-Knew-Where, Kentucky.

As soon as she opened the car door, she recognized the roar of rushing water.

"Is this a river?"

"Yep."

"Do we need a flashlight?" she asked, as he came around the car and took her hand.

"I don't think so. The moon's full."

And so it was. The earlier storm had left the area, leaving a mist in the low areas, the full moon playing hide and seek with a few remaining clouds. He led her along a paved path past a little building that could have been an office, or something, and through a park-like area. They followed another couple, who were talking and giggling ahead of them.

After a couple hundred yards, the woods parted, and she glimpsed the river ahead rushing past them, falling over a rift in the earth dozens of feet high.

"Wow," she breathed.

It was stunning. There was just enough light to see the water crashing and splashing its way from one level to another, swirling and pooling below before streaming away. Lesa would have loved to see the falls during the day, but the darkness gave the whole area an ethereal, fantastic aura.

She shivered, overwhelmed by the unknown coming at them from upriver, imagined being swept along with the current, off to distant places. It was both scary and exhilarating.

Brandon's arm wrapped around her, pulling her close against his warm, strong body. Safe and secure, but also anchored. For tonight she would ignore the tied-down feeling that always came with those sorts of thoughts. This was too magical.

"This is amazing," she whispered. "Thank you for showing me."

"Just wait," he told her. "This is cool, but—"

"There it is!" Someone from another group of people shouted, followed by a collective "Oooh."

"What?" she asked. "What's everyone seeing?"

"Come on." He pulled her along with him, moving away from the river and then back toward it, down a path that traveled over the cliff, approaching the river. She hadn't noticed it before and apparently most of the people above didn't know about it, because it was deserted.

But once they were about halfway down, closer to the water, Brandon stopped. "There." He pointed.

In front of them, rising from the mist at the bottom of the waterfall, was an arc of light.

"*Dios mio*! What is that?" Lesa breathed. She'd never seen anything like it in her life.

"It's a moonbow."

"Seriously?"

"No kidding. There are supposedly only two in the world, or somethin'. You gotta have a full moon and the right conditions, but it's just like a rainbow, except at night."

"Wow." They were silent for a few moments, watching the mist play with the full moon to create such a wondrous phenomenon.

Wrapped in Brandon's arms, feeling his heart beat against her back, the movements of his chest when he breathed in and out, alive and so focused on her. There was a real connection here between this man and this place—his home—and he was including her in that.

"Are you okay?" Brandon whispered. "You're shaking."

Oh hell. She *was* shaking. Because she was crying. Thank God it was dark here. This—this *feeling* stuff wasn't part of her plan. *Keep your eyes on the prize.* Faking a cough so she could wipe her face with the sleeve of her sweatshirt, she cleared her throat.

"Yeah. I'm fine. Thanks for showing me this." She unwrapped herself from his embrace. "Do you think we should get back to the girls? Your family will never forgive you if you have to reupholster the whole houseboat because they tore it up while we were gone."

She tried to ignore the puzzled look on Brandon's face as he followed her back up to the main path and on to the car.

• • •

A couple of romantically inclined frogs sang from the shore opposite the dock as Brandon and Lesa walked along the wooden planks toward the houseboat. She'd slipped her hand into his after they parked the car, and he admitted to himself that it felt good. Right.

"How you doin'?" He nodded to a familiar weekend resident walking a tiny pocket dog on a retractable leash. He'd have to wait a while to take Mabel and Maude for their evening constitutional.

"Your girls would have that dog for a snack," Lesa whispered, once they'd passed.

"They're actually terrified of him," Brandon told her. "The first time they met, Rex set up such a racket that Maude had an accident on the dock, and Mabel backed up so fast she fell in the water."

"Oh, no!"

"Yeah." Brandon laughed at the memory. "They were only a few months old then, and Mabel'd never been swimming before, so I wound up diving in after her."

"Eww," Lesa commented, looking down into the murky, oil-slicked water that lapped against the hulls of the boats. The water was clean and clear a few yards away from the docks, but the marina tended to collect all the nasty, floaty things and keep them close to the boats.

"Yeah. I had to shower three times before I felt comfortable enough to sleep."

"So what do you do here at night when you're not out on the lake?" Lesa asked.

"I usually sleep," he told her. "Not very exciting. Sometimes I read."

"Wow. You do live crazy, don't you?"

He nodded. "My parents and Justin used to stay up all night playing poker with the neighbors, but I'm not much of a gambler," he told her.

"Really? What were you playing for? Pretzels?"

"Mmmm, usually M&M's or Skittles," he said. "But sometimes they use real nickels and dimes."

"Oh, dear," she said drily. "I can understand why you'd be reluctant to gamble away your inheritance."

When she put it that way, it did sound dumb. "Even when I was little, I preferred to save my money instead of taking the risk of losing it." He shrugged. "But I always had enough for an ice cream the next day. Justin was always broke because he'd lost his allowance."

"So you would wind up spending all of your money, because you'd feel bad for him and buy him an ice cream anyway, right?"

"Maybe," he laughed. He pondered that for a minute. "Am I that easy to read—you already know what a coward and sucker I am?"

She bumped him with her shoulder. "You're not a sucker, you're generous. And you're not a coward—you're conservative. If you'd gambled, too, you might have lost, and neither one of you would have been able to buy ice cream."

Huh. He'd never thought of it that way.

But in a lot of ways, he was still a big chicken. Because he was such a sucker. Or at least he had been, once. He thought about his father's contention that he'd made enough amends for the situation with Suzanne. He might have helped Blue Mountain recover any financial hit they'd taken, but he wasn't done proving—at least to himself—that he was an older, wiser Brandon.

He looked at Lesa, glad that she was different. Yeah, she had her reasons for wanting to see Blue Mountain make a deal with her father's distillery, but she wasn't trying to finagle a special deal or steal company secrets.

They'd reached the boat, and Brandon had to release her hand to dig out the keys. It rocked gently as Lesa stepped onto the deck and gave another lurch when he came aboard. The sound of the water against the pontoon and the creatures of the night, along with the damp boating-associated smells, gave him a warm feeling of home. Whether here at the lake, at Blue Mountain, or just driving between the two familiar places, he was right where he wanted to be.

Having Lesa with him was— He stopped. Being with Lesa made it all that much better—or did being home make being with Lesa that much better? Or were the two things equal—

"*Hola*, handsome. We going inside?"

He shook his head and unlocked the sliding door to the cabin. Maude greeted them with a happy bark and wag and sat in a very convincing impression of a good dog. She must have—yep. The trash can contents were carefully spread across the galley floor. "Maude, dammit…"

Mabel raised her head from her place on the couch and looked at them guiltily.

"Mabel…" he warned.

She reluctantly unfolded herself and slunk to the floor.

"I'm gonna take you two out and let Rex get you."

Lesa laughed. "You take them out. I'll clean up."

"You don't have to do that," he said. What he thought was, *You can change into something more comfortable. Or nothing.*

She had moved within kissing distance, so he bent his head to hers and indulged in a little lip-to-lip libido resuscitation. Not that he needed it. He'd been on the edge of arousal all evening.

He grabbed her backside and pulled her against his burgeoning erection. Turning with her, he pressed her against the sliding glass door.

She slid her tongue over his bottom lip, taking a small nip, and then licking him again.

He could do this forever. Kiss her like this, over and over.

Although kissing led to touching. Which he was also willing to participate in. Sliding one hand under the hem of her top, he stroked the soft skin of her waist.

Damn.

"What the—" She pulled the phone from her pocket and glanced at the display.

"Do you need to get that?" Rhetorical question, to him. If the phone chimed, he answered it.

"It's Papa. I'll call him later." She pushed a button to silence the phone and shoved it back in her pocket. Reaching up to fiddle with his collar, she said, "Where were we?"

Mabel whined.

With a sigh, Lesa pushed him away. "Go. And when you come back, I'll challenge you to a Mexican game of chance."

He tilted his head at her. "Didn't we just have a conversation about how I don't like to gamble?" What did she have up her sleeve? The glint in her eye was decidedly devious.

"I think you'll like this game. It's called '*Poker el acto de denudarse.*'"

He tried to translate that in his head. "Is that strip poker?"

She grinned. "It's kind of a win-win game."

Boy howdy.

Chapter Seventeen

Lesa had barely finished sweeping up the last of the potato chip bag the dogs had decimated before Brandon was back.

"Wow. You must have had Rex scare the pee out of them to get their business done so fast," she observed.

He waited for the dogs to sit then unsnapped their leashes, giving each one an affectionate ear rub before straightening to hang the leads on a hook by the door. Such a good dog dad.

Uh, no. No thinking about whether or not he'd be a good kid dad. Because he would be, but not to her kids. She'd decided long ago that she had no interest in having kids. Maybe because she'd not had much of a childhood herself, what with spending most of it taking care of her mother, instead of the other way around.

So, she'd never make babies with this man. But she could pretend to be practicing. Because damn. The way his shoulders stretched that shirt, the long, strong arms, fingers, legs…

"Are you checking me out?" The sexy eyes, smile…

In two paces he was in front of her, his arms around her waist, hers around his neck. The very blood in her veins throbbed as he held her gaze and walked her backward. Down the hall. Toward the bedrooms.

As he shut the door behind him, she was vaguely aware of a whining complaint from the hallway, but ignored it when he pushed her gently down on the bed.

Kneeling in front of her, he pushed her legs apart and made room for his hips between them. The skin of her thighs tingled where his hands stroked, and she arched forward to make contact with his body.

He kissed her, his lips finding hers, tongues tangling then moving to run his mouth along her neck again and again, until she could barely think from the need swamping her senses.

While threading her fingers through his hair, the short silky strands tickled—a contrast to the firm grip of his hands on her.

He gripped her waist, holding her just a few centimeters from being able to press her core against him, and she ached with the need to feel his erection.

"Jesus, Lesa," he murmured, breaking the kiss long enough to stare into her eyes.

The emotion on his face was too much for her. Too honest.

"I—" He started to speak, but she cut him off with action.

Letting go of him, she pulled her top up and off, tossing it across the room in one motion.

His eyes darkened when he looked at her lacy bra, and she felt her nipples rasp against the fabric. He made short work of the clasp and slid it from her shoulders, dipping to touch his tongue to first one breast, then the other. She moaned when he took her into his mouth, feeling a tug between her legs in time with his pulls.

She tugged at his shirt, and he released her long enough to take it off, then leaned back in. But this time he put a hand on each shoulder and eased her down onto her back, running his fingers over her stomach and down to the waistband of her shorts. Her breath caught, and the movement allowed him to slip his fingers under the fabric.

Oh, God. Her body was on fire. She lifted her head to watch him. He was totally focused on getting her pants off. His tongue was tucked between his teeth, and she prayed he wouldn't bite it off before he used it on her.

The zipper slid down under his hands, and she lifted her hips so he could slide them the rest of the way off, along with her panties. The air hitting her skin did nothing to cool her off. She automatically pressed her legs together to ease the ache in her core, wanting instead to just throw them apart and beg him to *do* her, for God's sake.

One big hand landed on her stomach, and the other slid between her knees, pushing them apart. He was completely absorbed in her body, and she loved it. Loved how he gave everything he had to whatever he was doing. He licked his lower lip, and she felt the rasp of his tongue as though he'd already used it on her.

He approached slowly, his warm breath fanning her already hot tissues, soothing and adding to the ache at the same time like a million touches at once. He put his lips to her and explored every fold and nerve ending, around her entrance, just inside, then upward, around, and finally where she needed the most pressure, nearly sending her through the ceiling.

And then he began to stroke.

She managed to open her eyes enough to see him looking at her, holding her stare. The hand on her belly moved, stroking, and she put one of her own hands over it, holding on to him, because the tension rising inside her was about to be enough to carry her off this bed and out to sea.

The fingers of his other hand were between her legs, just around her opening, sliding back, rubbing over the outside of her back passage, and forward again. Not knowing exactly where he was going kept her unbalanced, distracting her from the orgasm that was trying to build.

"Shhhh, I've got you," he murmured, and she laid her head back, closed her eyes, and just *felt*. He was her anchor, keeping her safely in place even as he penetrated her defenses.

Just like that, without any buildup of straining, clenching muscles, she came.

Long and slow, rocking waves of pleasure soared from between her legs to her spine, along her limbs, and into her brain before pulsing back and starting again.

Over and over she came, until finally, she had to push Brandon's head away, lest she die.

Grinning, he kissed the inside of her thigh, then asked, "You okay?"

"I think so," she thought she answered. "Not sure I can reciprocate at the moment, though."

"That's okay," he said, reaching for a condom. "Can you just lay there and enjoy?"

"Huh? I thought that's what I had been doing."

He had the condom on and lifted her legs. Kneeling on the bed, he pushed himself inside her. His solid presence sliding into her, touching parts of her that she thought should be numb by now.

But that was not so.

As he slowly stroked inside of her, she began to move with him.

"No," she finally responded. "I can't just lay here."

"Well, if you insist…"

. . .

What he'd thought had been a light doze must have been actual sleep, because when dawn broke, Brandon opened his eyes and wasn't nearly as exhausted as he would have expected of someone who'd been making love all night long. He lay on his back, and Lesa snuggled into the crook of his shoulder, head on his chest, one hand idly stroking his skin.

"I really mean it this time. I'm never going to move again," she muttered.

"Yeah. Me, too." After a minute, he said, "I wonder if I could convince one of the dogs to bring my phone in so I can call the family and tender my resignation."

"What would you tell them?"

"I've discovered a new religion and am going to devote my life to worshiping at the altar of Lesa." He imagined the look on their faces if he did that. Brandon. He who always showed up to work early and stayed late, becoming a sex slave to a goddess.

"I like the idea of you on your knees," she said after a second, snuggling closer.

"This boat could be the church. With a congregation of one."

He thought he felt a slight shudder run through her, but then she laughed and said, "That's quite a change from the workaholic I met a few days ago."

"What? You don't think it would be hard work to keep you supplied with sex and devotion day in and day out?" He realized he was edging further from lighthearted post-coital banter to heavy relationship discussion—something she'd made clear was not on her radar.

Silence.

Yep, he'd gone too far.

One of the dogs whined pointedly and scratched at the door.

"Okay, girls." He groaned, rolling upright and searching for his pants. "I'm gonna take the dogs for their morning constitutional. You want anything while I'm up?"

"Are you going by the marina store?"

"I can."

"Maybe some coffee?" She didn't sound like she was going to stay awake to drink it, but he'd get it for her.

"You got it." He stood and zipped and buttoned and then slid into his flip flops. "Come on, girls," he told them, opening the door to two grinning, panting beasts.

The morning was cool and still carried a hint of moisture. Maybe it would rain more. He wouldn't be devastated to have to stay inside all day with Lesa, though she seemed restless in the houseboat—unless they were naked. Then she was every bit the free-spirited soul he'd come to appreciate. She'd really gotten to him, in spite of his best efforts.

In many ways, she reminded him of his early days with Suzanne—she'd been assertive in bed, too. But that was all an act, he knew. Lesa had already told him she was going to recommend that her father sign with Blue Mountain, so she couldn't possibly want anything from him but him. At least for as long as it lasted. He'd finally met a woman who'd gotten past his defenses, and she was bound and determined to move on as soon as possible.

Well, there was still a contract to sign with her father, and surely there would be opportunities for them to see each other in the future. Depending on how well the deal with the tequileria worked out, he might need to travel to Mexico a lot in the future, and he bet he could manage to show up whenever Lesa just happened to be visiting her father.

Mabel pulled Brandon's left arm in the direction of the marina store, while Maude tugged the other direction, toward the grassy area next to the boat ramp.

"Business first, ladies," he told them, giving in to Maude's preferences.

Funny. Brandon didn't feel at all divided about being here with Lesa right now. Every other time he'd been here, he could take it for about a day, then he fired up his laptop to check in with Blue Mountain. He had no desire to do that right now. He just wanted to get Lesa's coffee, go back to the boat, and crawl under the sheets with her.

Leading the dogs to the marina store, he saw that the CLOSED sign was still turned out. *Oh well*. They could come back later for coffee.

. . .

After Brandon left, Lesa dozed for about thirty seconds, her mind wandering to the previous night. Wow. They had really rocked each other's worlds. It scared her how easily she could get used to this.

She allowed herself a brief fantasy of a life with Brandon. Marriage. A house. A baby. Just like his parents and just like hers.

Opening her eyes, she looked at their tiny stateroom. There was about a foot between the bed and the wall on one side, and no space at all on the others. *Yeesh*. How could anyone spend an entire vacation here? Twenty-four hours and she was ready to climb the walls—which didn't have far to go to close in on her.

Her fantasy was overwhelmed by memories of her parents. Her mother in that bed for years while Papa worked his behind off to pay for the hospital bills, while Lesa spent those same years taking care of Mama. Her entire childhood. Papa telling her that family takes care of family—he had to work, so she had to help Mama.

No, she wasn't going to let history repeat itself. As appealing as Brandon was, he was a family man with a distillery. There was no doubt in her mind he would never give that up. She was not ever going to get stuck taking care of anyone—parents, children, or dogs while her husband worked eighty-hour weeks.

Her phone buzzed. With a sigh, she felt around on the floor until she found it.

"*Hola*, Papa," she said.

"Lesa, where are you?"

"I'm…in Kentucky. Where else would I be?" She pulled on one of Brandon's T-shirts and began making the bed.

"I received a contract from Blue Mountain."

A frisson of excitement ran through her. Yes. This was what she'd been hoping for. Waiting for. Help for PZ and her ticket to freedom. "Did you sign it?"

"I did not. The terms are unacceptable."

Oh, no. "Why? What's wrong?" She had to find a way to fix this, to make it happen.

"He wants too much for what he's giving us."

"Well, Papa, he's got to make a living, too," she pointed out. The bed made, she moved into the kitchen and started to fill the sink to wash the few dishes they'd used.

He let loose with a string of curses that turned the air blue.

"Papa, I really think you should take this. Give it a year, like they suggest, and see how next year's tequila turns out. Then we'll know if it's worth it." She scrubbed a plastic promotional cup so hard that the logo, for whatever company gave it away, began to come off.

"I'm not going to sign anything unless we get a better deal. That's what you're there for, isn't it? To make sure that our interests are taken care of."

What? She thought she was here to make sure everything was on the up-and-up, and she'd done that. What was he suggesting? She thought about spending another year at Pequeño Zarigüeya, running tours for people who were only interested in free samples of the final product, and her heart clenched.

Not happening.

She had to make sure this went through. She rinsed the cup and put it on the drainer, reaching for another. "Okay, Papa, don't worry. I'll find a way."

A noise drew her attention away from the sink. Brandon and the dogs stood just inside the sliding door. Oh, hell. What had he heard?

· · ·

Brandon had only caught the tail end of her conversation— "*Está bien, papá, voy a encontrar una manera.*" He thought she was telling Papa she'd go do something tomorrow, but his Spanish was shaky at best.

The expression on her face when she saw him standing behind her, however, told him that her conversation wasn't something she'd wanted him to overhear.

The recently melted crystals of ice that had encased his heart for so long began to gather in his gut.

Fucking Suzanne, all over again. No, he wasn't going to go there. He was just paranoid because Lesa had been a little distant earlier when he'd made a joke about long-term stuff.

She smiled, holding her hand up, mimicking drinking and raising her eyebrows at him in question. "*Hey, Papa. Te llamaré más tarde. Yo también te amo.*" She pushed a button and put the phone down on the counter. She stared at it for a moment before looking at Brandon.

"No coffee?" she asked, twisting the fingers of her right hand with her left. She was nervous.

Damn.

"The marina shop was still closed. What did your dad want?" No point in getting unhinged. There wasn't really anything she could steal at this point, was there? He was Brandon Morgan, steely calm marketing executive—not the naive kid who let a woman take advantage of him.

She waved his question away. "Oh, nothing. Just checking in."

"Okay." Until he knew what was going on, he'd play along. Maybe he was wrong. God, he hoped he was wrong. Carlos should have gotten his proposal by now, but Lesa didn't mention that.

She smiled and sashayed over to him and wrapped her arms around his waist. The heat of her body was simultaneously arousing and irritating. This wasn't the action of a woman with her lover, it felt like a woman on a mission. "What did you have in mind for today?" she asked.

He had the sensation of waiting for the sky to fall, so he opted for his comfort zone. Work.

"Actually," he told her, "I hate to say this, but I think we need to head back to Blue Mountain. I checked my email a little bit ago." He held up his phone to show her that he'd taken it with him to walk the dogs. "And it turns out there are a few things I need to take care of."

"Okay," she said a little too brightly. She let him go and began gathering their things.

Chapter Eighteen

Lesa stayed quiet most of the way home from the lake. She'd been tempted to suggest another cruise. Avoid reality for another few hours—days, even. But something had changed when Brandon returned from his walk. She knew, from the way that he kept checking his phone, that he was anxious to get to Blue Mountain and get his hands into his real life.

That was fine. She needed to get back and have some time to figure out what to do to convince Papa to take the barrel deal. She'd felt claustrophobic on the houseboat without Brandon that morning—the weather, the tiny rooms, hell, even the wallpaper reminded her of being trapped in a life she didn't want. But after she'd hung up from talking to Papa, the whole world felt a little too tight. She had no idea what he expected her to do to make this deal acceptable to him.

Her mind and heart were full of Brandon Morgan. The hours she'd spent here with him—having a little vacation in the middle of her obligations, making him laugh, seeing him take off the mantle of responsibility he wore like one of his ever-present Blue Mountain polo shirts—she was all jumbled up about it. He made her feel things…

She'd never considered making room in her life for a man, especially not one who was so…permanent. She was going to travel the world and take care of no one but herself. No responsibilities, no pressure.

It didn't matter, anyway. There was no way he'd ask her to stick around, even if she were so inclined. He'd been talking with post-orgasmic endorphins running around his brain earlier this morning, and then he'd gone all workaholic on her, reminding her why she wanted out of the distillery life to begin with.

She'd tried to talk to him for a while on the drive back. Asked questions about business—what more could a guy like Brandon want to talk about than work? But he was monosyllabic, so she gave up.

As the car turned up the long drive toward the big log house on the hill, her heart gave a lonely lurch.

The weight of impending doom that Lesa had felt building all the way from Lake Cumberland was justified when she spied Papa sitting in a rocking chair next to Brandon's grandpa on the front porch of their log home.

"Oh, *mierda*!" All of the air in her body got stuck and she gasped like an *axolotl* out of water.

"What?" Brandon had been watching where he was going, but now slowed and looked where Lesa's attention was drawn. "Is that—is that your dad?"

"Yep."

"What the hell? You didn't tell me he was here when he called this morning." He pulled around the house.

"I didn't know!" What was he up to? "Papa hasn't left Pequeño Zarigüeya in…in forever."

"Huh." Brandon shot her an unfathomable glance.

"With my luck, he got Tia Rita to do some Mexican crystal ball gazing and found out we went off the mountain alone."

Leave it to Papa to find a way to keep her in check.

"Ah." He seemed to ponder that for a moment, then shook his head at some internal thought and smiled. "Do you suppose he'll believe me if I tell him we stayed in separate houseboats?" He scratched his jaw.

"Sure. And I'll tell him I got this beard burn from letting the dogs kiss me."

Brandon looked at her carefully. She knew he would see her chapped lips—who knew that so much kissing was hard on your mouth?—and the rash that had yet to fade from this morning's glorious make-out session.

God only knew what she'd look like trying to walk up the stairs to the porch. She hadn't had that much sex in...ever, and she'd used muscles she didn't know she had.

"Well," he said, "I can always pretend you ditched me for some cigarette-boat-owning show-off from Tennessee or something, as long as I don't take off my shorts and share the scratches on my ass."

Lesa snorted, and finally, *finally*, the tension that had grown between them over the past few hours eased.

"Okay," she said, taking in a monster yoga breath and letting it back out. "I'm an adult. I'm allowed to get naked with anyone I choose."

Was that a growl coming from Brandon's side of the car? It was. He tried to cover it with a cough, but she'd definitely heard something. She tried not to smile with pleasure. She was going to miss the hell out of him when she was off in the middle of wherever she wanted to be doing her thing. She could admit that much without compromising her life plans.

As though reading her mind, Maude stuck her head over the back of the seat and laid it on Lesa's shoulder with a sigh.

She reached for the door handle to face Papa's music, but before she could get it open, Brandon grabbed her other hand.

"Hey."

She turned to face him, trying to recover the light mood, but he was sober-faced, searching her face for…what? Something she couldn't give him, she was afraid.

"I had a good time. Thanks for coming with me." He rolled his eyes. "I mean—well, yeah. Thanks."

"Me, too," she said, and meant it. Both ways. "I know I may never see you again after this week, but I want you to know how much I enjoyed being with you."

"Lesa!" Papa pulled the door open before she realized that he'd come down from the porch.

"What's going on, Papa?" Lesa asked. "Is everything okay?"

"I don't know," Papa said, eyeing Brandon. "I have some…questions. About the proposal."

"Okay," Brandon said. "Ask away."

"Perhaps you would care to get into the house first?" Papa suggested.

Brandon looked as though he wanted to protest, but then shrugged and carried their bags up the stairs.

"What is it, Papa? Why are you really here?"

Her father scowled. "I was worried when you told me that we should take this deal without giving me any solid reasons. I can see from the look in your eye that you are starry-eyed for this Brandon. You can't have a rational opinion."

"I can, too!" She didn't bother to deny that she was, at least temporarily, over the moon for Brandon Morgan.

"Tell me why you are so sure that he is reliable. I will not let my only daughter be hypnotized by lust into telling me things that she *wants* to be true."

"Oh, for heaven's sake, Papa. Everything that man does is for his family's business!"

Papa's eyes flared. "Exactly why he won't be fair. You need to make sure that what he does is for our business!"

"You mean you want me to try to…*influence* him to

change his offer?" Lesa couldn't believe she was being asked to do this.

His eyes softened. "Our Pequeño Zarigüeya is all we have left of your mother. I am not willing to spend so much of our money on a risky proposition."

"What is the offer?" Maybe she could…what?

"He is only willing to give us half of his barrels and wants full market price up front."

"And what do you want?"

"You mean, what do *we* want? This is for Pequeño Zarigüeya."

"Sure." She tried not to scream with frustration. Any time she'd suggested that she didn't want anything to do with the tequileria in the future, he completely ignored her.

"I want all the barrels at a fifty percent discount, to be paid after the tequila is aged." Papa crossed his arms over his chest.

"Did you even ask him yourself to change the offer?"

"Oh, I will," he told her. "But I look at that boy and I don't think he'll budge for me. For you, he'll change the direction of the sun."

Lesa snorted. That was ridiculous. Oh, *Dios*. Please let it be ridiculous.

She thought longingly about a slow walk around the Eiffel Tower—alone.

With a sigh, she said, "I'll talk to him if you don't have any luck."

• • •

Brandon looked through the kitchen window at Lesa and her father in the driveway. He wondered what the hell they were up to. As he watched, her shoulders slumped in the universal body language for heavy sigh, but then she squared her shoulders and said something to her dad as she walked toward the house. What was going on?

When they were in the car just a few minutes ago, and he looked in her eyes, he believed there was no way she expected to see her father here, and he questioned why he'd mistrusted her earlier. Their discomfort with each other faded a bit. She might be acting weird because she was leaving soon and was pulling away in preparation. Whatever her dad was doing here wasn't helping.

"Hey, you're in the way," his mother said, bumping him with her hip so she could get to the sink, her hands full of asparagus. "Go ogle your girl somewhere else. And take these bags out of here."

"Love you, too, Mom." He kissed her on the cheek and she swatted at him as he hoisted the bags and left the kitchen.

"Brandon, wait!" It was Carlos, coming in the back door with Lesa. "Do you have a minute?"

"Sure. Let's go in here," he said, leading the older man into the dining room. "This is our temporary boardroom, until the new tasting center's finished. What can I do for you?"

"I want to discuss the terms of your proposal," he said.

"Hey, y'all." Grandma stood in the doorway, her ancient red-and-white polka-dotted apron neat as a pin. "Supper's gonna be ready in five minutes. Go wash up."

"We have some business to discuss first," Carlos told her.

"Bullhockey. Go wash."

Carlos was silent, clearly shocked that Grandma was so demanding.

"Sorry, sir. But when Grandma says it's almost suppertime, we don't argue." His mouth twitched.

"Now," Grandma said.

"*Sí*," Carlos said and went.

Lesa, following Grandma, smoothly snatched her bag from Brandon's hand and winked at him on her way past, so he followed her. She stopped at his room and turned to give him one of her smiles—the kind that spoke of the hours they'd spent making love and made Brandon willing to sit up and beg.

He dropped his bag next to hers—he'd have to take it into Justin's room in a minute, but for now…

"Hey," he said, leading her inside and then putting his hands on either side of her, trapping her against the door. Her orange and lime scent wafted up to him and he breathed deep, lowering his head to feel her silky hair against the side of his face, kissing her on the shoulder. "You wanna maybe go for a walk later?"

Her hands walked over his abs, and he nearly groaned, wanting her to touch him lower.

"So did you and Papa come to terms about the proposal?" she asked, her lips against his neck, kissing him, then running her teeth along that tendon on the side.

Oh, Jesus. When she did that, he couldn't think. Didn't want to think. But she'd asked a question. The proposal. *The proposal.* His ardor cooled slightly.

"Uh, not yet."

"Well, shoot. I was hoping that you'd have it all sewn up nice and tight so we could talk about what comes next."

What comes next? He thought she wanted nothing to do with Pequeño Zarigüeya.

"What do you mean?"

"I don't know," she said, stroking her hands farther down his stomach, resting on his belt. "Whatever the future holds." Was she talking long-term future, or immediate?

A knock on the door behind her head made them both jump. "Hey, bro. Time for grub." Justin. Perfect timing as usual.

"Okay, we're on our way." Then, with a quick kiss to Lesa's beautiful mouth, he adjusted himself, hopefully enough to not embarrass everyone when he walked into the dining room, and opened the door.

Chapter Nineteen

The enormous oak kitchen table overflowed with people when Lesa arrived. Papa sat amidst Brandon's family. His mom and dad, grandparents, Justin, and all three McGraths— Allie, Eve, and their mother, Lorena.

Brandon pulled out one of the only two remaining chairs for her next to Allie and seated himself next to her father.

"I didn't get to spend as much time with Lesa when she was a little one as I should have," Papa was saying.

That was an understatement.

"Why not?" Grandpa asked. He didn't seem to have any qualms about nosing in where he wasn't wanted.

But Papa answered him. "Her mama was sick. I worked all the time to make enough money for the treatments. Lesa was a good little nurse, though, and took very good care of her."

"Well, now, that's too bad," Grandpa said. "You shoulda maybe hired some help. No wonder the girl's got such a hankerin' to see the world."

"Grandpa," Justin interjected. "Can you pass the None-of-Your-Business Peas? What did you put in these, Grams? They taste a little like Let's-Change-the-Subject."

"You hush, boy." Grandpa waved the mood-lightening subject change away. "So what's the situation now? You ready to make a deal with us and move forward?"

Carlos looked at Brandon's grandma, who nodded her permission.

"I guess, since you're company, you can talk business," she allowed.

He nodded. To Brandon, he said, "I don't like your proposal."

"What don't you like about it?"

"I don't like anything. Your terms are unreasonable."

There was silence as everyone in the room waited to hear what Brandon would say.

A moment of something—panic?—crossed his expression, but then he cleared it to become the cool, calm businessman that Lesa knew him to be.

Oh, please let this work out, she silently prayed.

"Can you be more specific, so we can see if there's common ground?"

"Item one. I want all the barrels."

Brandon shook his head. "You don't have enough tequila for all of them this year. You can't leave them sitting around until next year, they'll dry out."

"That doesn't matter. I don't want anyone else to use what is for my exclusive use. You could otherwise sell the others to my competition."

He pursed his lips and his forehead furrowed in thought. "We can add a non-compete clause, or if you're gonna pay for them, I guess we can probably find a way to make that happen."

"I'm only paying for the ones I fill with tequila, and I want them on consignment, to be paid when the tequila is sold."

"Absolutely not." Brandon crossed his arms across his chest.

Carlos nodded, as though he'd expected this. He pulled a sheet of paper from his pocket and handed it to Brandon.

"What's that?" Brandon's grandpa asked.

"It's a bid from another company." He named a well-known mass-production distillery. He read it, then handed it to his father, who looked at it, with Justin and Grandpa looking over his shoulder.

"This is not a good deal," Brandon's father said.

"It seems to me like a better deal than you can give," Carlos told him smugly.

"Nope." Brandon was adamant. "For one thing, you won't get exclusivity. They are too big. And their materials are crap. These guys don't use the best. Or even the middle best. Half of the barrels will leak before the end of the first year."

"They have guaranteed replacements for any bad barrels." Carlos waved away Brandon's warning.

"But not the product that you'll have lost."

"Maybe it's a risk that I'm willing to take."

"I'm sorry, Carlos," he told the older man. "Blue Mountain's survival doesn't depend on this deal."

"But your relationship with my daughter does."

The sound Lesa made was buried amidst the collective gasp from the women at the table.

But the look that Brandon gave her stood out more sharply than anything she'd ever witnessed. The hurt, the confusion, and then…the anger.

All of her plans evaporated with a hiss. "Brandon—"

"You played me." He nodded, as though this made perfect sense. "Okay. Well, I kind of knew that." He turned away from her, shutting her out. To Carlos, he said, "I think you should go ahead and take the other offer."

Through the cacophony in her brain, Lesa was vaguely

aware of Papa making some sound of protest. "Lesa, you have to talk to him," he said. "You were supposed to fix this."

"Are you kidding?" She stared at her father as though just now seeing him for the first time. She should have expected something like this. All of those years she'd given up to help him before she did what mattered to her, and this was what she got. Blame when things didn't go his way.

Brandon still wasn't looking at her.

Okay, fine. She knew what to do now. What she'd always wanted. Screw them all. She stood. "Mrs. Morgan and Mrs. Morgan," she said, speaking to Brandon's mother and grandmother. "Thank you for your hospitality, and while I'm sure that dinner is lovely, I'll be leaving now."

She stood and pushed her chair back under the table while the silent, shocked people around it looked on.

"So." She heard Grandpa say before she and Papa left the kitchen. "What did you say was in those peas?"

Chapter Twenty

"We're sorry for the delay, but we've got the mechanical issue resolved, and flight twelve-ninety-seven to Paris will begin boarding in five minutes." The cheery voice on the loudspeaker was a harsh contradiction to the dozens of complaints that had been rising in number and volume over the past hour and a half in the gate area at John F. Kennedy Airport, where Lesa waited to start the next phase of Operation Single World Traveler.

It had to be better than phase one, which consisted of a gorgeous spring weekend in Manhattan. She'd walked for hours, covered Central Park on foot and in a horse-drawn carriage, been to the Empire State Building, the Statue of Liberty, and the 9/11 Memorial. She'd seen a Broadway play and eaten a donut in front of Tiffany's at three in the afternoon. It was breakfast food, if not breakfast *time* at Tiffany's. But it didn't count, because she didn't have anyone to share the joke with.

Damn it. This wasn't going the way she'd expected. Her whole life she'd been planning for this. See Pequeño Zarigüeya in good financial shape, leave Mexico, visit New York City —

do all the touristy things—and then start on Europe.

She'd finally shaken off the weight of her childhood—the smothering responsibility for everyone and everything— her mother, her father, Pequeño Zarigüeya, and then, even Brandon. Because surely what had been between them would have become more of the same—expectations she didn't want to have to meet.

Instead, she'd taken on a different mantle. Guilt.

She hadn't left Pequeño Zarigüeya on stable ground. She'd been reminding herself over and over again that she didn't owe anyone anything. She'd promised her dying mother that she'd look out for her papa and help him when she could, but the statute of limitations should have run out by now. She'd done her share.

So why did she feel so terrible? Why was she so worried that everything was screwed up now, and Papa—and Tia Rita and Raoul—would be homeless soon?

"Excuse us." A woman with a large black dog wearing a red vest brushed past her and sat in the only empty seat, which was right next to Lesa. The woman was clearly blind, because she was the only person in the room who didn't see the ugly aura that surrounded Lesa.

The dog, some sort of Lab mix, stared at Lesa and panted.

"No drooling on people," the woman told it.

"It's okay, I like dogs," Lesa said, and promptly burst into tears.

"Oh no. Here," the woman said, patting in Lesa's direction and shoving a tissue into her hand. "I'm sorry. We'll move—"

"No, don't move," Lesa wailed. She was drawing attention to herself, but she didn't really care. "I miss…" She trailed off into another bout of sobs.

"You miss your dog?" the woman asked. "Seamus is supposed to be working, but since we're just sitting here, it's okay if you want to pet him."

"I don't have a dog," she said, but still reached out to stroke the Lab's silky ears.

"Okay…"

Gathering herself, she blew her nose and wiped her eyes. Great. Mascara everywhere. Taking a deep breath, she tried to explain, but it came out garbled. "There's a man. And some dogs. And then my father showed up and I told them all to go to hell, and now here I am, about to start the adventure of my life."

"Uh huh."

Lesa looked up, expecting to see that whole "Okay, step away from the crazy lady" look on the woman's face, but instead got a sympathetic smile.

"So this man, you love him but he doesn't love you?"

"Oh. No. Actually, I'm pretty sure he was starting to fall in love with me. I left him."

The woman nodded. "Ah. Your father didn't approve."

"No, I think Papa would have liked me to be with him. But that's part of the problem. If I was with the guy— Brandon—then Papa would keep using me to try to control what Brandon does."

"And Brandon is willing to do whatever you say?"

"Not at all. See, he was in love with this other woman one time, and she took advantage of him, and I'm not going to do that, and he wouldn't have anything to do with me anymore anyway because he thinks I was using him to—" She broke off, not making any sense to herself anymore. "Never mind."

"Well," the woman said, "I don't know about everything you're telling me, but if this guy really cares about you, he'd be willing to look at your side of the story. Love is blind, you know." She elbowed Lesa and laughed. "That was a joke. Love is blind? Get it?"

Lesa smiled. "Yeah. I don't know. He was pretty mad. And I'm not supposed to want to be tied down, and he's the tying down type, you know?"

"Has he told you that? That he wants you to do exactly what he wants?"

"No." And he hadn't, she realized. When she'd told him about her dreams to travel, he'd been interested, never pooh-poohing her thoughts.

"Is that where you're going now? To try to fix things?"

"Flight twelve-ninety-seven to Paris, first class passengers can begin boarding now," the cheery voice announced to a collective shuffling and gathering.

"You know what?" Lesa said, standing and picking up her backpack, "I think maybe I am."

The woman, who had also stood, smiled and held out her arms. Lesa hugged her, this complete stranger. "You go get him," she told her.

"Thanks. I will. But I have to go take care of some other stuff first," she said, then went to find a ticket agent to try to change her flight to Mexico.

. . .

Brandon threw a Cheeto into the water and watched a couple of ducklings fight over it. The mother duck quacked at them from the other shore. Probably telling them they were going to turn orange if they ate too much of that crap.

He looked at his fingers, stained with cheese powder, and held his hand out for Maude to lick clean.

On the other side of the little dock, Mabel ignored everything, contentedly gnawing on — what the hell was that?

"Mabel, whatcha got there?" He stood and walked to the dog, seeing something that might have once been shiny, and — it was Lesa's shoe. One of the pair she'd given the dogs when she'd come to Blue Mountain.

Damn.

He'd avoided coming to the lake for a while after she left because he couldn't face memories of her that would confront him in every crevice of the houseboat, but Grandma and Grandpa wanted to come down this weekend, and he'd drawn the short straw.

He looked around to find something to trade with Mabel, but there were no chewy bones. Giving up, he dumped the rest of the cheese puffs into the water and sat back down, watching the lake evaporate.

Grandpa groaned as he sat down in the chair next to Brandon. "How long you gonna wait before you go after her?"

"Who?" He knew exactly who, but he wasn't going after anyone, so it was a moot point.

Grandpa was silent.

Brandon sighed. "She was just using me."

"Well," Grandpa cackled, "being used for sex isn't the worst thing in the world. Your grandma's been using me for the last fifty years and I'm still moving along pretty well, except for these knees. She's got to be on top more often now, because—"

"Ugh! Stop!" Brandon clapped his hands over his ears. When it seemed safe, he lowered them again.

"What was it that she did, exactly?" Grandpa asked when he'd stopped laughing at Brandon's response.

"She tried to get me to change my proposal to Pequeño Zarigüeya. Just like fu—uh, freaking Suzanne."

"No. Not like fucking Suzanne," Grandpa said. "Suzanne was a liar and a thief and a man-eater. Your girl just got a little distracted from what's most important in life."

"She had a dream. She needed to get that deal between Blue Mountain and Pequeño Zarigüeya done so she could go travel the world and be independent and alone."

Grandpa harrumphed. "Dreams change. Maybe you should check in with her and see if she's having a change of heart."

"I don't think so."

"Why not?"

"Because…" Because it hurt too much to think about what might have been. Because he didn't want Lesa to feel beholden to him, even if he could find a way to make a merger palatable to Carlos and his fragile ego. Because he didn't want to see her face and know that he could never touch it again. "Because I burned that bridge with Carlos, and it would just be too awkward."

"You're a lily-livered chicken." Grandpa told him.

"Better than a kudzu-brained toad," Brandon shot back, laughing, but the truth was, he was afraid to get burned again.

But fear was never going to get him anywhere. If he'd let fear and shame run his life, he never would have managed to help Blue Mountain get where it was now, a rising force in the bourbon industry.

"Possum hockey," Grandpa spat. "I heard that Carlos's deal with Big Bourbon fell through, and he's back where he started. He might be willing to reconsider, if you do. You know as well as I do that this company is as solid as a rock. We can afford some speculation."

"I don't speculate."

"I know."

Maude stood and shook, collar jingling and ears whapping.

Mabel gave a soft woof to greet Grandma, who'd come out to stand behind Gramps.

"Maybe you should give it a shot."

Maybe he should. Sitting here feeding the ducks processed cheese powder wasn't doing anything for him or the environment. "Shit."

Grandma smacked the back of his head.

"Sorry. But I've got to make some calls. Can I — "

"Leave the girls here. Go."

Chapter Twenty-One

"Welcome home, Lesa." Tia Rita bustled through the door of the Ruiz house carrying six tote bags of…what did she have in there, anyway? Food usually, but even her plump aunt didn't need that much food for one day.

"*Hola*, Rita. *Cómo estás*?"

"I'm good," her aunt said, hugging her. "I'm glad you're home. Carlos has missed you. Where is he?"

"I don't know. He said he had a meeting this morning."

"A meeting? How mysterious." Rita began unloading grocery bags into the refrigerator.

And it was. She'd been home for three days, and Papa kept taking off to go to meetings he wouldn't tell her about. When he was home, he was greeting tourists and even participating in a few of the tours, which the guests loved. And he'd been asking Lesa's opinion about some ideas he had for new bottles he was considering. Should they go with a cheaper bottle, and a fancier label? It would save money and appeal to new drinkers, but would they lose their existing customers?

"He didn't tell me where he was going, but I suppose it

was to the bank."

She was afraid it might have something to do with the fact that Papa had been totally bluffing when he'd shown Brandon that proposal from the other distillery. He'd made it all up to get Brandon to come to his side of things. Well that certainly hadn't worked out, had it?

She'd come home to help Papa one more time — to convince him to do something differently before Pequeño Zarigüeya went under. She wanted to go to Brandon, but she couldn't. Not until she'd made things right with Papa.

The sound of a diesel engine grinding up the hill reached her ears, followed by the faint, tinny sounds of a mariachi band leaking from the windows of the bus. "Oh, here comes the next tour group." She stretched her neck and prepared to get back to her old job. She'd agreed to stay a little longer, just until she could get someone else trained.

A lizard dropped from the branches of a tree to snatch a flower from the plant at her feet. "*Hola*, Mabel," she told it. "Where's Maude?"

Stupid. She'd named the lizards after Brandon's dogs. They were unlikely to ever rub up against her to ask to be petted and didn't greet her with whuffles and barks. Of course, they also didn't chew up her accessories, either.

The bus screeched to a halt outside of the gates of Pequeño Zarigüeya, and Lesa pasted on her best smile. She did love to introduce the tourists to her family's tequila, and she was going to enjoy her job now, for as long as it lasted.

"*Hola!*" she called out, shoving the squeaky gate open.

The people filing off of the bus and into the courtyard were not like any resort or cruise ship patrons she'd ever seen. At least, not since she'd left Kentucky.

"Hey, Lesa," said Justin Morgan, turning to help his grandmother down the last step of the bus.

"Um, hey, Justin. Grandma Morgan. Mrs. Morgan. Allie.

Mr. Morgan, Grandpa Morgan...Mrs. McGrath. Eve." She looked, but the sun glinted off the windows of the bus and she couldn't see if anyone else was going to come out.

The familiar pair of feet and black pants weren't who she was expecting, though, since the first souls off were all from Blue Mountain. "Papa? What's going on?"

Papa avoided her gaze and stepped out onto the hot stone path, but he was smiling.

And there he was. Her Brandon. Khakis and a polo shirt. That had a...was that an opossum? Yes. Instead of an alligator, or the Blue Mountain Bourbon logo, he had an opossum over his left pec. She checked. They were all wearing them.

He approached her warily, but he needn't have been worried. Her heart filled nearly to bursting when he reached out to hand her a shiny gift bag. She reached inside and pulled out her very own Pequeño Zarigüeya shirt.

"What's all this?" she asked.

"Meet our new partner," Papa said proudly. "Pequeño Zarigüeya is now part of the Blue Mountain family of distillers."

"This is what your meeting was?" It was a rhetorical question, but she was beyond words at the moment. She'd been expecting Papa to come home with an eviction notice or something, and instead he brought her—a family.

He brought her Brandon. Who stood in front of her, a hesitant smile on his handsome face. That sweet little scar next to his mouth.

"I was going to consult you, but then I decided to surprise you," Papa said, sheepishly. "You have been so sad that I wanted to give you a gift."

"Uh..."

"I know you promised your mama that you would help me with Pequeño Zarigüeya, and you only wanted to see Pequeño Zarigüeya successful so that you wouldn't feel guilty leaving me to struggle alone. But I wanted you to stay, so maybe I didn't try too hard to make things better, and I nearly lost you both because I didn't trust you to make a good decision. Now you have a choice."

"I don't understand."

But Tia Rita, who had followed Lesa outside to see what the holdup was, chose that moment to burst into tears, and Papa held his arms open to his sister, who blubbered on his shoulder like a toddler.

• • •

As Brandon took in the sight of Lesa, her hair pulled behind her head with a big turquoise clip, her shining eyes and soft, smooth skin, he was more certain than ever that he'd made the right decision. Even if she rejected him, he was doing the right thing.

"I need to sample some of this ta-kill-ya right about now," Grandpa said, shoving past him and grabbing Carlos by the arm. "We all need to be sure that this stuff you make here is the real deal."

With that, the whole Blue Mountain posse left Brandon and Lesa alone in the hot afternoon sun.

A lizard shot across the courtyard.

"Where are you going, Maude?" Lesa asked it.

"Maude?"

She grinned. "Yeah. She's got a sister named Mabel. They keep eating Tia Rita's flowers."

"That's awesome." Did that mean maybe she missed him, just a little?

"Yeah. I thought it was kind of lame, but now maybe not so much?" Her black eyes sparkled.

They were silent, and he just looked at her.

He took a deep breath. "I've done a lot of thinking," he

began.

"I'm sorry," Lesa interrupted. "I'm so sorry for the way I did—what I did."

He nodded and prepared to eat some crow. "You didn't do anything wrong."

"I didn't mean to. But I knew your history with that woman, and I made you think that—"

He shushed her with a finger over her lips, those beautiful lush lips. "It's okay. You know what you made me think?"

"What?" She was a little breathless.

"You made me think that all work and no play makes for a boring Brandon. You made me think that it's okay to take a chance now and then."

She smiled then. "You made me realize that caring about someone doesn't mean you have to let them smother you."

They stared into each other's eyes.

"You are so wonderful," she said.

A grin crossed his face. She thought he was wonderful. But still. "So anyway, you have a choice now."

She shook her head, putting one hand up, as though to touch him, but then letting it fall again. "Papa just said so, too. How so?"

"You can do whatever you want. Your dad's comfortable with the agreement we came up with. Finally." He rolled his eyes, which made her laugh. "It took a few meetings, but we decided that we'd accept a third ownership of Pequeño Zarigüeya in exchange for exclusive barrel rights and help with some of your infrastructure issues. And once Pequeño Zarigüeya is back on its feet, you can buy the stock back. Meanwhile, we share in the profits. If you agree, then we'll sign the papers. Your life is your own. You can do all the traveling you want to do, and you don't have to worry about your dad or Pequeño Zarigüeya."

He said that last bit with as much fortitude as he could

muster. He felt like a damned bumper sticker on the back of a 1970s Volkswagen Beetle. *If you love something, set it free…*

"This doesn't sound like the decision of a careful businessman like you."

"I know. I don't usually like risk. I'm not interested in wasting money on horses, cards, or zipline adventures designed to part me from my money. Turns out that I have a secret wild side." He moved toward her, putting a hand on each side of her waist. "When I was with you, when you came to Blue Mountain, I felt really alive for the first time in years. Work wasn't my everything."

"I—"

He rushed on before he forgot what he wanted to say. "I'm not asking you to come back to me, to come live at Blue Mountain or anything else you don't want to do. This investment in Little Possum is for me. I want to diversify, and I can afford to make some mistakes if it doesn't work out. But I think it will. I have some great ideas. You don't need to have anything to do with it, if you don't want to. You don't ever have to see me again. We need you to sign some papers at the bank because you're the legal heir, and your father needs to know that you'll be taken care of if something happens to him."

She smiled and took the hand that was shushing her into her own warm palms. "So I don't have to come back to you for this deal to happen."

"That's right." He swallowed and forced himself to be still, not to drag her up against him and kiss the living daylights out of her.

"And I don't have to live at Blue Mountain."

"Of course not." He hadn't meant to say that part. She'd live there with him in his heart, he figured, for a long, long time, but—

"I want to make sure that I'm not confused. My English

seems to be failing me."

He snorted.

"So I *can* come back to you if I want? And I *can* come to live at Blue Mountain?"

His heart, already beating way too fast, sped up. "Uh, yeah. That's what I'm saying. I don't—I don't want you to feel pressured, though. This"—he waved around him, indicating Little Possum—"this is purely business."

"I don't know," she said. "If you're going to be participating in a company that's partially mine, I think I'd better come around and keep an eye on things." With that, she slid her hands around his waist and pressed against him, looking up into his face.

"Can I kiss you?" he asked, still a little uncertain if his brain was understanding what his heart and body wanted to be true.

"Brank, if you don't kiss me, I'm going to have to tell my Papa that you're being mean to me, and he doesn't like it when people mistreat his little girl."

When she called him Brank, he knew everything was okay. Okay right now and in the next few minutes after that. What happened later? He'd worry about that when later got there.

After a long, slow kiss that promised more to come, Lesa pulled away.

"So. What are we going to call this new entity? Blue Possum? Or Little Mountain?"

Epilogue

A pigeon snatched the piece of baguette that Brandon dropped on the ground and then flew away, only to be accosted by another, bigger pigeon.

"They're not being very nice to each other," Lesa observed, sipping her wine. The Eiffel Tower over her right shoulder added just the perfect note to the prettiest picture he'd ever seen.

"Don't move," he told her and grabbed his phone to capture the image.

"You're going to have to go somewhere and upload all of your data before you run out of space," Lesa told him, laughing.

Before he could snap the photo, his phone vibrated with an incoming call. He sighed.

"Aren't you going to answer that?" Lesa asked, rubbing her foot along his calf.

He snorted. "I'm on vacation. Let it go to voicemail."

She snatched it from his hand and looked at the screen.

"You better get this one."

He took it from her, and seeing that it was his brother—who never called anyone unless he was desperate—pushed the answer button.

"Dude." Justin's voice was loud and clear over the thousands of satellite miles.

Even clearer were the sounds of Mabel and Maude barking in the background.

And then there was Allie. "Dammit, Justin, I don't care what you have to tell him. Lie. Tell him Grandpa won the lottery and is threatening to buy the country club and turn it into a nudist colony. Tell him the still house blew up. Tell him—"

"What's wrong?" Brandon was on high alert. He and Lesa had been in France for three days, and he wasn't ready to go home. To either of their homes. They were splitting their time between Mexico and the U.S. these days, and he was perfectly comfortable in either place, because he could work—and play—from anywhere.

"Dude," Justin repeated.

"Dude," Brandon responded. "What?"

"I need you to come home and get these dogs. We're done babysitting."

"Are they being bad? Just give them the remains of Lesa's sandals. That usually settles them down."

"It's not that."

"Then what? Are they sick?"

"No, It's Allie. I mean…"

"What's wrong?" Lesa immediately keyed into Brandon's mood and leaned in, trying to listen.

"What's wrong with Allie?"

"Nothing. I mean—"

"Justin. You're freaking me out."

"Oh, for God's sake," Allie said, obviously taking the phone from her husband because her voice was the clearer, stronger one.

"I wanted to tell him," Justin complained in the background now.

"Tell me what?"

"We're pregnant."

Brandon dropped the phone, and Lesa scrambled to pick it up. She took over, getting the details from Allie while he stared at the birds, imagining his reckless, big, tough brother as a dad. Which would make him an uncle.

He took the phone back from Lesa. "When is this going to happen?" he asked.

"In about five months, give or take." The excitement in Allie's voice was infectious.

"It's a boy! A boy. Do you hear me?" Justin shouted in the background.

"Yeah, bro. I think all of Paris heard you."

Lesa wiggled with excitement and hugged Brandon. "That's so awesome! I mean, if it's not going to be a girl, it's good that it's a boy, right?"

He laughed and kissed her. "Yes, it's good."

"A boy!" Justin was still hooting in the background.

"God, Justin, it's just a dick," Allie complained.

"But it's a really good dick!"

"Is everyone okay, then? Allie, you feelin' good?" Brandon asked.

"Yeah. I'm good. Tired. Which is why you've got to come get these dogs. They're driving me crazy."

Brandon grinned. "I don't know," he told his sister-in-law. "If you expect any babysitting from us, you probably want to bank some hours in advance."

"Brandon, I think Maude's in heat. You can come home and get her, or I can turn her loose. I saw the Beckers' Chihuahua sniffing around her yesterday afternoon."

"Hey, babe?" He looked at Lesa. He could sit here and

watch her feeding pigeons for as long as she kept rubbing her foot along his calf, but then again… "You want to see if you can get our flight bumped up a day or so? I think we need to get back to Blue Mountain."

"But the baby's not due for months yet!" she protested.

"Yeah…I have a feeling that if we don't get a move on, there might be a few puppies arriving way before then."

"Let's go. Now." Lesa stood and began gathering their things.

"You don't have to break any speed records," he said, rising more slowly. "I think we have time to pick up a few extra pairs of fancy gold sandals before they start teething."

Acknowledgments

Many, many people had a hand in this project. Fortunately, this isn't an Academy Award speech, so I'm not going to get cut off by the orchestra...

Thanks to Nicole Resciniti, for saying, "What about bourbon?" when we were brainstorming this series. And for answering all of my psychotic freak-out emails and texts with patience and kindness. You are the bomb.

Everyone at Entangled, especially Liz and the Heathers for being so awesome and supportive. I love this job!

Extra especially, Robin Haseltine, for the amazing editing marathon. I promise, I'll throw no more babies out with the bathwater. Oh! And thanks for going to Cozumel on that cruise so you could tell me all you learned.

Speaking of Mexico, kudos to Frank and Marta Kroger, for also getting married twenty-five years ago so you could go on the "research trip" with us, and you know, being willing to taste all that tequila.

Cecy Robson for consulting on Latino culture. Even though the original concept changed enormously from when we first spoke about it, I suspect Lesa might look a little like you.

Patrick Clouse, aging warehouse manager for Buffalo Trace Distilling, for answering all of my questions. The fact that I ignored many of the answers to make the plot work is my own doing.

Jessica Lemmon, Kathryn Miller, Angela Dennis, Stacy McKitrick, and Rachel Klink for reading and brainstorming.

Very grateful for Kim B and my Monday night home-peeps for keeping me sane (ish).

And as always, thanks to my favorite family. I love you!

About the Author

Teri Anne Stanley has been writing since she could hold a crayon—though learning to read was a huge turning point in her growth as a writer. Teri's first stories involved her favorite Saturday morning cartoon characters, followed by her favorite teen idols. She has also authored a recipe column (The Three Ingredient Gourmet) and scientific articles (guess which was more interesting!). Now she writes fun, sexy romance filled with chaos and havoc, populated by strong, smart women and hunky heroes.

Teri's career has included sex therapy for rats, making posing suits for female body builders, and helping amputee amphibians recover to their full potential. She currently supplements her writing income as a neuroscience research assistant. Along with a variety of offspring and dogs, she and Mr. Stanley enjoy boating and relaxing at their weekend estate, located in the thriving metropolis of Sugartit, between Beaverlick and Rabbit Hash, Kentucky.

Find love in unexpected places with these satisfying Lovestruck reads...

PROPERLY GROOMED
a *Wedding Favors* novel by Boone Brux

When Joya Bennett wakes up after her brother's wedding, half-naked and lying next to her lifelong crush, she's mortified. Intending to lay low and housesit for her brother until the embarrassment fades, she sneaks away before he wakes up. Lincoln Fisher doesn't do relationships, but if he did, his friend's little sister would be the one to tie him down. And now they're stuck in the same house. For two weeks. She's off-limits. And he needs to keep it that way, even if the heat building between them is hot enough to blow off the roof...

IN A RANGER'S ARMS
a *Men of At Ease Ranch* novel by Donna Michaels

Former Army Ranger Stone Mitchum doesn't have time for sex. He's too busy running a construction company and transitioning veterans back into society, but when Jovy Larson falls into his arms, his libido snaps to attention. To prove she worthy of taking over her family's company, she's trying to sell gluten-free, vegan food—in the middle of cattle country, Texas. But by the time her lease runs out and the test is over, she's faced with a new challenge...competing against Stone's sense of duty to win his heart.

ONE SEXY MISTAKE
a *Chase Brothers* novel by Sarah Ballance

Olivia Patton's all about her one-night stand with sexy hacker Grady Donovan—until an epic snowstorm shuts down the city and thwarts her morning-after escape. Now that they have to *talk*, all hell breaks loose. Grady and Olivia can't stand each other. If it wasn't his apartment, she'd shove him outside to freeze. But with all the blistering sexual tension flying around, a second night with the hacker might be exactly what she needs...if they don't kill each other first.

LOVING HER CRAZY
a *Crazy Love* novel by Kira Archer

Iris Clayton is supposed to be on a tropical island. Instead, she's snowbound in Chicago overnight. Good thing there's a hot cowboy to keep her company—a cowboy that can make her tremble with one sultry look from under his well-worn hat. Montana rancher Nash Wallace had no idea roaming the city could be so fun—or illegal. Now he's falling hard and fast. Wanting to spend his life with someone after one night is insane. Except, nothing has ever felt so right, and neither of them wants the night to end...

Discover the **Bourbon Boys** *series...*

DRUNK ON YOU

Also by Teri Anne Stanley

ACCIDENTALLY IN LOVE WITH THE BIKER

DEADLY CHEMISTRY

CPSIA information can be obtained
at www.ICGtesting.com
Printed in the USA
LVHW090405270222
712100LV00002B/287